NATE PERKINS

THE WAY CITIES FEEL TO US NOW

AND OTHER STORIES

The author would like to acknowledge the fine publications and kind editors that first gave these stories a home. "The Way Cities Feel to Us Now" originally appeared in *Timber Journal*, "An Unfolding" in *Decomp Magazine*, "Ms. Pac Man" in *Noncanon Press*, "Log" in *Pure Coincidence*, "Los Huevos del Señor" in *Triquarterly*, "The Last Time I Almost Had a Threesome" in *Pithead Chapel*, "Lemons" in *Potluck*, "I Can Sleep Here" in the *Philadelphia Secret Admirer*, "Put Me on a Dog Leash and Make Me Eat Taco Bell off the Floor" in *South Broadway Ghost Society*, "What Fucking Up Feels Like" in *Maudlin House*, and "I'm Sorry Your Boyfriend is in the Mental Hospital Again" in *Keep This Bag Away from Children*. "Acknowledgment" was originally published as a chapbook from *Pest House*.

"In the West there are people who believe in its landscapes and cities like a secret cult. Nate Perkins lets you into this world of travelers, the secret passwords that allow you into the Western Lands."

-Noah Cicero, author of *Give it to the Grand Canyon*

"Coming to you from the front lines of the crusty underbelly of American weirdness, Perkins writes from a place of hard-earned material, and these stories brim with authoritative detail. He knows the sordid basements of punk house parties as well as he knows the grandeur of the Utah desert landscape. All of it told with humor and sadness and deep empathy for the lost and broken-hearted heroes of this monster of a motherland."

-Bart Schaneman, author of *The Silence is the Noise*

"Depression makes most people's memories collapse inward onto themselves. Perkins struggles with himself but knows the beautiful punctures on the the stick-and-poke world around him."

-Brendan Wells, of *Uranium Club*

maudlinhouse.net
twitter.com/maudlinhouse

**The Way Cities Feel To Us Now
and Other Stories**
Copyright © 2019 by Nathaniel Kennon Perkins

Cover by: Rachel Pfeffer

Table of Contents

New Beginning Spell for Ally

I told you that I write spells, little stories for people that I
never send to them.

And that I think about the intended effects of these spells for
months after writing them.

Wondering if the person I wrote the spell for is happy.

If she still thinks about me.

If the spell worked, or if it will take effect soon.

But what I told you was a lie.

I don't write much of anything anymore.

Pyramid Blues

I am a cottonwood tree for being sad. I spread out my roots and wait in vain for the Rio Grande to flood like it used to.

As a cottonwood tree, I throw my backpack in my 1991 Dodge van. After a false start in which I can feel the sickening pressure building in my temples and have to turn back for my medication, I light out, spreading my roots west from my west toward Gallup, where I don't remember ever having been before. On the way, after I get through Interstate 40's desert storm and shout with joy at a good luck sign in the form of a full double rainbow over a red rock butte, I pick up two hitchhikers. Young kids, just 21. Scott and Dave from Davenport, Iowa. They both wear tie-dyed t-shirts. Scott gives me a big grin and starts talking about all the weird places the pair have slept in the past few days. Dave hangs out quietly in the back. He has a black eye, but I don't ask about it. They've both read *On the Road* and *Into the Wild*, and more than anything they want to do the road kid thing, but they aren't yet quite sure how it works. I share my cigarettes, green chili cheddar bagels, and my most valuable travel knowledge. Temporarily forgetting my sadness, I take shameful joy in the knowledge that these are two new people that listen to what I have to say, do it eagerly, even. They don't know me, but they understand that what I'm saying is mostly correct.

It is because they don't know me that they listen.

Maybe it is precisely in the newness of this not knowing where I retain some meager value.

Maybe I am the first celebrated piñon nuts gathered by ground squirrels before they've eaten so many that they are sick of the taste, before there are so many piñon nuts in their den that they don't even want to look at them anymore. Their den has a big kitchen, but they never wash the dishes or wipe down the counters, and I, thinking that I'm proving something by enabling them, will do all the chores.

I stop and make the hitchhikers get out and jug for gas. I teach them how to do it. They walk up to people at the pumps and say, "Excuse me, ma'am. Could you spare any gas? We're trying to get to Tempe, and really anything would help."

A man, pockmarked and in a dirty stock-car racing t-shirt, recently kicked out the convenience store for being just this side of falling down drunk, staggers over to us. He says he'll pay us ten bucks to go in and buy him two packs of Camel Silvers. Scott does, and when he comes back out the bum is furious.

"I wanted two four-packs of Steel Reserve, motherfuckers!"

The bum tries to climb in my van but I grab him by the t-shirt and pull him back out again. He falls onto the broken, oily asphalt. I don't want to be a dick, but it's not my fault he fell down. We've got a full tank now, and there's no fucking way I'm driving this guy anywhere. We take off.

Not until we are down the road a ways do we realize that we still have the two packs of menthols, plus the ten dollars. Guilty, we quietly rejoice and smoke them.

I am the dried out shell of a desert tortoise, picked clean by turkey vultures and sun-bleached white for loving you. Giving away my cigarettes, and sweeping up the butts later. I am the tortoise right before death, before desiccation, pissing away my last liquids in fatal fear.

This is my first time driving down the Beeline Highway. A few inches of snow cover the ground where the road's elevation is at its highest point, and in this snow are panicked tire tracks that lead off the narrow highway and a minivan, which has taken a nosedive into a ditch. At the bottom of the canyon is hail and lightning over the Phoenix Valley, making me think that the world has probably ended. Somewhere in between these two sights there is more gas jugging.

I definitely recognize the man who is considering my plea. He doesn't really want to give me gas, but he wants to think of himself as a nice person. Worn white shirt and ugly tie. Scuffed leather shoes. My age or younger with a wife and baby in the pickup.

"Are you Mormon?"

He says he is, and I say I am too. He looks at my tattoos and piercings. He smells the stale smoke of cigarettes, but I tell him I was a missionary once, and he fills my red plastic jug with five gallons.

I pour it in the tank, and we get in. The van won't start. It's turning over, but not getting gas. I think about how the plugs are new, the distributor cap is new, the fuel filter is new. I'm not a mechanic, but it's probably the gas pump. I've learned enough about automotive repair from watching YouTube to deduce that much. I also know enough to know that I can't fix it myself. I can't drop the tank. I curse. Get out. Get back in.

By some miracle, the van decides to start.

Jesus Fuck.

The hitchhikers have never been to Tempe before, so I let them out on Mill Street, where I know they will be able to panhandle enough for a few beers, and probably meet some dirty kids who can show them somewhere local to sleep.

I have been to Tempe exactly three times, and I never know where the fuck I am, but I always end up in Tops Liquors on University and Farmer. I don't really even drink anymore, but I find myself there again, just wanting to pick up some smokes and a bottle of wine and some condoms because I think that *I* might actually be the one who gets laid tonight.

I am a fucked up lizard, some kind of skink without his tail, for thinking so often about how much sex you're having.

I buy smokes and wine and condoms, and I remember the first time I was in this liquor store. My friend's band, Solid Attitude, was on tour. My friend was and is straightedge, but the rest of the band wasn't, and I wasn't, so we loaded up on booze. The cashier said he had to check on something in the back real quick, so Mickey, the singer, walked out with his arms full of bottles, and we drove away.

I think about drinking the wine with the woman I am going to being staying with. I met her the first time because she came to one of my readings when I was on tour. It was in the creepiest shittiest anarchist house I've ever been in. I'm a shitty, creepy anarchist, but this place really gave me the willies, although this lady was cool. I ran into her again at Albuquerque Zine Fest, and she told me that the house had burned down under suspicious circumstances. I wasn't the least bit surprised. I had mentioned that I had been thinking of heading out to Arizona soon and asked if I could stay with her for a night.

I want to push myself out of my comfort zone. I want to make myself start talking to people I don't really know, and she seems like a good place to start. She is a writer and a punk. She is Indonesian and has cat-eye glasses. She is older than I am. She is probably the slutty kind of feminist.

But the van won't start. The miracle has expired. It has been pushed aside by something else.

She is drunk when she picks me up. I throw my backpack in her car, but I forget the wine, leaving it in the van, which is going to stay in the liquor store parking lot overnight.

Her friends and housemates are also drunk, and we stay up late smoking cigarettes and listening to stoner metal records. This guy Josúe talks to me about cumbia and country and western. Later, the zinester tells me that she has a serious drug problem and is broke and finds it annoying to have to remember when people use they/them pronouns.

I sleep on the couch.

In the morning, I hear her and Josúe fucking. I hear an ass being slapped, and he comes with a caveman grunt.

I am the seeds of a prickly pear that have been shit out by desert creatures for thinking that I was going to get laid.

She is late for work, so Josué drives me back to the liquor store. We listen to chicha. The underside of the flipped up bill of his hat says "cabrón" on it. He leaves me in the parking lot.

There's an O'Reilly's auto parts store a half-mile away, so I walk there and buy a fuel filter and some cheap tools and walk back. One of the themes of traveling for me (at least within the United States) is that of constantly smelling like gasoline, no matter how hard I try not to or how much I wish that I didn't. I'm lying on my back now, sandwiched between the filthy surface of the liquor store parking lot and filthy underside of my van, struggling to loosen the hose clamps that connect the fuel line to the filter. When I finally do, gasoline comes pouring over my face and my t-shirt. I wiggle out and wipe my hands on my jeans.

Cigarette break.

I half hope that I will go up in flames like a Vietnamese monk.

I suspect that everyone who smokes cigarettes feels this way from time to time.

I throw on the new fuel filter and tighten everything up. Another cigarette for good luck, and I put the key in the ignition. Still nothing.

Two hours later, I'm in the lobby of an automotive shop in Chandler, handing over my key, and hoping to God that they won't soon tell me that they need to replace the fuel pump.

The guy behind the desk looks at me and says, "I gotta be honest with you, guy. We're pretty backed up right now."

"How backed up?"

"You're, uh"—he looks at his computer screen—"eleventh in line. We're not going to get the diagnostic done 'til after lunch."

"Do you think she'll be running by tonight?"

"Depending on what it is, yeah. Tonight or tomorrow morning."

When I ask him if I would be able to sleep in the van overnight if it has to stay at the shop, he looks at me with that mix of disgust, pity, and admiration that I have come to relish, and he says, "Yeah, probably, depending on what state it's in."

If the van was in the state of New Mexico, I'd be sleeping in my bed with you. Instead, I walk out of the shop, checking out the rooftop access on the surrounding buildings, trying to figure out if any of them would be good places to sleep if worse comes to worse. The whole Phoenix Valley is a strip mall. I look at this part of the strip mall and think about how you're sleeping in his room tonight.

Over the next few hours, I eat a burrito and use the Wi-Fi at Starbuck's to download pornography from The Pirate Bay so I can watch it later when I don't have an internet connection, maybe even while I'm waiting to fall asleep on a rooftop in Chandler, AZ.

The mechanic calls to say that it's the fuel pump.

I give him the go-ahead and hang up and try to pretend like I'm not spending the last of my money. There's maybe one grassy patch within a mile. I find it and lie down.

It doesn't seem like it right now, but I am trying my fucking hardest to get my shit together. In a couple weeks, I will be 29 years old. I'm not calling my mom to ask for money. I swear that when I get back to New Mexico I will start looking for a job that's not just writing papers for college students. Writing papers for college students is an okay job—I'm my own boss—but it's not the kind of job that a person who has their shit together has. I rest my head on my backpack and close my eyes.

The sound of the sprinkler heads popping up from the ground wakes me, and I make a break for the sidewalk, cursing and wondering if someone turned them on on me on purpose, but before I can start feeling too sorry for myself, the shop calls. My van is fixed.

God, the next hours are embarrassing. I drive to a Wal-Mart parking lot, where I pull shut the window shades and watch a porno called *Real Amateur Hotwives and Cuckold vol. 6*, and I masturbate.

Then I gas jug and panhandle at a Chevron until I have a full tank of gas and $30 cash. Folks in Chandler drive nice cars and are very kind. They seem surprised by my panhandling, like they had forgotten that panhandling exists and I am giving them a pleasant and thoughtful reminder.

I take the money to McDonald's, where I try to wash the smell of gasoline off my hands. Teenage employees flirt with each other behind the counter and get my order wrong. So I do something bad: I eat meat. Not because I want to, but because they accidentally give me sausage instead of egg (I have been a shitty vegan lately. You and I used to bond about being good vegans, but now that we aren't, we don't talk about it anymore). I smell like gasoline. I have recently masturbated in a Wal-Mart parking lot. I begged for fuel and the money to buy the meal. I really, really don't want to ask another human for another thing, so I eat the meat.

For eating meant, I am the creosote that is choked out by cheatgrass and red brome because of grazing in the West. I am the slowest elk.

There is no real meatiness to the meat. It doesn't taste like anything.

Because I don't know where else to go, I drive back to Tempe and park in front of Tops Liquors. My van is starting to get messy. There is a mountain of empty packs of cigarettes between the front seats. Empty gas station coffee cups and Red Bull cans are spread all over the place.

I go back and forth about being bitter and bummed and mad. College students come in and out of the liquor store, and I think about javelinas bedding down together in the dirt and shitting all over the place.

Tanner is a dude I know from the internet. He lives in Tempe. He is a writer and a skateboarder, and the same small press distros our zines. I have never met him IRL. He doesn't get off work until 10:00.

As a non-javelina, I decide to walk around Mill Street and see if I can find my hitchhikers. This crusty kid tries to spange me, and I ask if he's seen them.

"Two young kids? Were they wearing tie-dyed t-shirts?"

"Probably. Yeah."

"I saw them a while ago when it was light out."

I look for them some more, but instead I see hordes of frat guys and then a beautiful girl with blue hair. We lock eyes for a few seconds. I am wearing my cool leather jacket. I don't try to talk to her. My hitchhikers are probably hanging out by Tempe Town Lake under one of the bridges. My hitchhikers are burrowing owls, squatting the desert.

When Tanner gets off work, we meet at Cornish Pasty to drink Schlitz and trade stories about panhandling and flying signs and breaking into buildings to sleep in them and being cold.

Punk shit.

He once crashed a sailboat into some rocks on the Mississippi River during a blizzard and had to be rescued by the fire department. I once was a day late hiking back from the Alexander Supertramp bus in Alaska, and my aunt called Search and Rescue. We both had gotten on the news for these things.

Two ladies join us. One of them is Tanner's old college girlfriend, and the other is her friend, a 30-year old virgin dental hygienist.

Pretty quickly, it seems like Tanner and the college girlfriend are going to hook up. There is no circumstance in the world in which I would hook up with a virgin who hates guys with dirty teeth.

I haven't really been drinking since my last birthday, but now I have had two beers.

I recently read a zine called *I Quit Drinking & I Hate You All*. I identified with it in a real way, and it made me sad.

We decide to go to another bar, called Casey's, before last call. On the way over, Tanner and the virgin dental hygienist start yelling at each other, probably because the dental hygienist thinks Tanner is a scumbag because the college girlfriend is currently married to someone else and has an eight-month old baby. I'm not hip to the intricacies of what's happening, but Tanner jumps out of the car before it is parked, and I follow.

"Inside bar. Stat," he says. He buys me a Budweiser and a shot of tequila, and now I am feeling drunk for the first time in a year.

The bar is packed, and there's no way to know where the dental hygienist and the college girlfriend ended up.

In the huge mess of partiers, we run into Tanner's most recent ex-girlfriend, and he introduces me. She is polite, and then awkward, and then Tanner and I stand about five feet away from her and talk about partners and ex-partners and try to decide whether monogamy or polyamory is more bullshit. I don't want to be a javelina. I am not a California condor that mates for life. I am not a kangaroo rat that fucks all the other kangaroo rats, either.

Tanner and I are bummed out, but at least we are bummed out together. We drink our Budweisers and smoke cigarettes.

The bar closes and we are packed in someone's car with a bunch of people I don't know. Then I am in my underwear in an apartment complex hot tub. Someone is telling me to talk more quietly because the neighbors will get mad. There is a British steel worker who came to the U.S. for the first time to watch an NFL game, and somehow he ended up in a hot tub with all of us. The fact that we are a bunch of punks and don't know anything about football is frustrating to him. Also, everyone keeps asking him about Harry Potter.

I am talking to this badass woman named Riley who is a helicopter mechanic and rides motorcycles. She has a bunch of tattoos and is wearing a small bikini. It turns out that she is Tanner's roommate.

Tanner's most recent ex-girlfriend shows up, and I can tell

that shit sucks for him, so we get ready to go. In the apartment complex parking lot, Tanner kicks his skateboard really hard into a curb, and Riley, looking as though she genuinely loves him, tells him to chill out and pick it up.

Riley drives me to my van, and I follow her to their house, where we sit on the back porch and talk about serious shit. At 5:30 I go to sleep. It sucks to sleep in a van in Phoenix because even in November the city doesn't cool down at night.

When I wake up, I feel like shit. I am a mostly dead rattlesnake stretched across the section of Historic Route 66 that leads to our house for how sorry I am.

I really am sorry.

Sorry that these things I say I've worked through and forgotten keep coming back up over and over again.

Like being mad about the night of our fifth anniversary.

Like feeling resentful that I am the one who has to take care of us

(Coming home late at night from my shitty job at the Hilton Garden Inn, walking through the snow and smog in the bad part of Salt Lake City that we lived in, feeling freaked out because the same guy in the street offered to sell me hard drugs again, and opening the front door to find you and him drunk and high and laughing, and I didn't know where the rent money is coming from. That was before you two were fucking, but back when I could see that you both wanted to, but didn't know that the other one did too. Back before I knew that you actually Loved each other).

I am lying in my van, hot and overextended and hungover. I am sorry.

This is the day where I maybe get the best compliment of my whole life. What happens is that I wake up before everyone else, and I drive away, but in the Filiberto's parking lot (I have enough panhandling money left over for a country burrito), I realize that I've lost one of my shoes. A few text messages later, I figure out that it's in Riley's car, so I meet the whole crew at this smoothie place a couple miles away. I'm hanging out on the sidewalk talking to Tanner. Riley is inside the smoothie shop with their other roommate, a girl whose name I can't remember.

When the ladies walk out, Riley says that the girl at the smoothie counter had asked, "Are you two with those guys out there?"

Riley: "I told her that we were, and she just nodded and said, 'they match you.'"

That I, some hung-over, sad sack of shit wearing only one shoe might "match" these beautiful women (a helicopter mechanic!) seems like the kindest thing that anyone could ever say. I suspect that the girls might not feel the same exact way about this statement, but I try not to think about it too much.

For no reason at all, I am one of the wild horses that live on the Colorado/New Mexico state line between San Luis and Questa.

High desert, low life.

I get my shoe and I drive to Tucson.

If Phoenix is usually hell, then Tucson is the chillest heaven, and I'm happy to be driving through the saguaro pearly gates. I've always had good luck in Tucson, or at least luck that doesn't seem so bad in retrospect.

I follow Google Maps to my friends Jasper and Kit's new house. It's this little boxy thing right next to the train tracks.

Jasper has a long history of letting me sleep in a van in front of her house.

It started in January, 2015, when you and I were in Tucson for the first time. A Wal-Mart security guard had kicked us out of the parking lot, so we were wandering up and down Fourth Avenue and trying to figure something out. On one corner there was a Bluebird short bus painted all black and with Earth First! stickers on the back windows. Maybe halfway down the block were some shitty guitar and banjo buskers, crusty kids, obviously a couple traveling together in a black Bluebird short bus.

When they finished their song, I asked, "Hey, where can you park that thing to sleep in without getting hassled around here? Are there any safe spots?"

They gave each other a look that said they thought I might come kill them in their sleep if they gave me the geographic coordinates I would need to make that possible.

Before they could come up with a polite and safe way to tell me, probably a serial murderer of punk rock runaways, to fuck off, a voice piped up from the crowed of onlookers.

"You can sleep at my house if you want."

It was a skinny kid with thick glasses and big boots and dreadlocks down to her ass.

"You have to promise not to rob me though."

That kid was Jasper.

That night, we played Magic: the Gathering, drank port wine, and listened to This Bike is a Pipe Bomb. There were a bunch of nights spread out in the years that followed, but that night was the first.

You haven't come with me to Tucson any time since then.

Jasper and Kit are standing outside with their dog, named "Mo the Dog," and their cats, "Kitten" and "Easy." Also, there's a tall, nice-looking kid with a braided rat-tail. I don't know him.

I meet him: Hunter.

A bunch of stuff happens now. Hugging, coffee, a tour of the house and the garden, a whole bunch of stuff. Somehow (my processing of the events that lead us there is hazy), we end up walking down some railroad tracks, trying to sneak into the second night of a music festival called Night of the Living Fest.

Jasper and I are standing by the back fence, right outside of the backstage area. Inside, Mike Watt is playing. I'm nerding out. I have to get in there.

I wait until a train goes by, and then I scramble over the fence as fast as I can. The horn blasts and the rumbling on the tracks drown out the sound of my 215 lb. body slamming into the chain-link, and I'm over. I duck into a portapotty and lock the door behind me. I wait for a vague, reasonable-seeming amount of time before coming back out again. Then I walk toward the general admission area, follow a member of some band through a gap in the fence, and I'm watching Mike Watt! The Man in the Van with a Bass in His Hand!

Jasper gets caught jumping over the fence, and Kit has homework to do, so they text me to say that they're headed home.

After Mike Watt, I see Seth Bogart, Reigning Sound, Nobunny, Shannon and the Clams, King Kahn and BBQ

Show, and Big Freedia. It's a weird and pleasurable line-up for sure: the person who invented twerking and a bunch of bands that make me feel nostalgic for 2009. Back then, when I was still doing punk and garage music fanzines, I could have written a thousand tedious pages about Night of the Living Fest, but I'm not much of a music critic anymore.

The show is good.

I have a nice time.

I walk back to Jasper, Kit, and Hunter's place.

I sleep in my van.

Trains roll by all night, but they don't bother me at all.

It's only recently that I am consistently able keep myself from getting back into bed, or even get out of bed at all, for that matter. When I first started taking Zoloft, a couple months ago, before the dosage was dialed in, I didn't feel like killing myself anymore, but I still stayed under the covers and watched Netflix all day. Now I know the secret. Getting out of bed in the morning means breakfast burritos.

Breakfast burritos are as good a reason for living as anything.

Jasper, Kit, and I go to Tania's 33, which is definitely one of my top three favorite burrito joints in the entire Southwest. This means something. If you know me at all, you know that I know my shit when it comes to the Southwest, and I really know my shit when it comes to burritos.

The burrito I order is *fucked* up. Tater tots, soyrizo, and nopales. Thank Satan for the Sonoran Desert.

Jasper is stressing because she is playing a set at a rave this upcoming Friday, the night before she has to take the GRE. Kit is talking about how they would totally be a professional sub (not in the sense that they want to teach middle school kids, but in the sexual sense: black bandanna, right pocket) if they weren't so scared of being murdered by cis-men.

Kit: "When I turned 18, my friends wanted to get me a birthday present, so they set me up with a local dom here in Tucson who runs a video company. She does really cool work, but the production esthetic is so late-eighties/early-nineties. Anyway, she and her partner were going to pay me to do a video session, and when they found out I had *just* turned 18, they offered me a fuck ton of extra money to be in the video. There was some girl there who, like, wanted to try out subbing but wasn't totally sure about it yet, so she was just watching. She ended up being locked in a cage in the background the whole time. I think I have photos still. I think they're on my Google Drive. What are you grinning about? Oh yeah, here they are."

In the photo, Kit is wearing a ridiculous platinum blond wig, and their gaudy bedazzled pink butt plug matches their bellybutton piercing.

"That lighting is incredible," I say.

Later, I take a shower and get dressed in fancy clothes to go to my friend Christian's wedding, which I had almost forgotten was the whole point of coming to Arizona in the first place.

The shindig is being held at a fancy ranch in the foothills below Saguaro National Park. Christian's a rich kid, and I think his wife Meredith is a rich kid too, but they're good people.

In high school, Christian and I played in ska bands together. We fell out of touch for a while, but reconnected last year because I traveled to Seattle a couple of times, once just for fun and once when I was on tour. He lives up there in a sailboat on Lake Union.

I hit the bar first thing. I haven't really been drinking lately, but I'm 30 minutes early, and a bunch of people I don't know are standing around. I get a Dos Equis and wander out into the cactus to smoke a cigarette.

When I walk back in, I am surprised to run into Andy Conrad and Evelyn Hernández—now Evelyn Conrad—two friends from high school that I probably haven't seen in seven or eight years. I try not to ever think about high school too much. I feel like I probably had a good time while it was happening, but looking back on it gives me panic attacks that no amount of sertraline can dominate. It seems like six lifetimes ago.

Andy, Evelyn, and I take seats by each other.

"Where's your wife?" Evelyn asks.

You hate that word. You prefer "partner."

"She had something come up and couldn't end up making it." I change the subject. "When would have been the last time that we all saw each other?"

Evelyn digs her phone out of her purse and pulls up a photo of the three of us. We all have dorky glasses and are dressed up for something. My face is shaved, and I don't have any piercings or tattoos. We are grinning in a goofy, sober, and sincere way.

"Where was that?" I ask.

"Uh, I think that was at Christian's last wedding," she says.

Sure enough. That one was at a fancy place too, somewhere

in Salt Lake City. I distinctly remember leaving the door to the dining hall open so that the peacocks would wander in and shit on the floor while everybody was eating dinner. I remember driving home at 100 miles per hour afterwards so I could make it to a movie (one of the Harry Potter movies maybe?) with some other friends.

I start to remember those friends, and then I start to remember high school.

I remember holding hands with Evelyn at a punk show.

I wonder if Evelyn remembers. I wish I had another Dos Equis.

The ceremony starts.

Wedding are nice. This one is nice. The officiator's microphone isn't loud enough, and Christian's dad talks about Jesus and the Bible. During the vows, one of the bridesmaids faints. Once everyone has finally settled down, Christian and Meredith kiss and look very happy. I head back to the bar and then out into the cactus for another smoke.

Andy, Evelyn, and I sit at the same table at dinner, along with a bunch of Christian's rich Seattle friends who I have never met before. Everybody keeps asking whom the empty seat beside me is supposed to be for. I act like I'm as confused as they are.

I think about our wedding. How we served pizza and your grandpa read a Walt Whitman poem. I think about the "coarse smut of beasts." I think about my best man and wonder if in five years, on the night of Christian and Meredith's anniversary, Christian will drive home from a lowbrow art opening in Santa Fe while his wife and his best man stay in a hotel room and fuck each other.

I ask the waiter to bring me another beer, and I am a gila monster, black and orange and venomous and living in a crag between two rocks.

Andy is talking about smart phones with one of the Seattle tech bros. Evelyn is telling me about how cute their three little boys are. Christian's dad gives a toast and says a bunch of shit that makes me cringe. I drink champagne. They cut the cake.

I think about high school more. I can't help it. Another thing I remember is that there was a pizza place, unfortunately named "American Pie," just down the street from the school. Andy and his twin brother Tim were the first ones to start going there for lunch because the manager was their older brother's friend, and he would only charge them 75 cents instead of a dollar for a slice. Word got out about this great deal, and I started going to American Pie with them. Soon, however, the manager became wary of how many kids were showing up every day with Andy and Tim to get a cheap slice, and the special discount was revoked if anyone other than only Andy and Tim came. Don't ask me why. Seems like a pretty dumb business move.

Shortly after this happened, I went to meet the Conrad twins at our usually spot by the gym doors, but they weren't there. I waited for a few minutes, and then walked over to American Pie by myself. They were sitting at an outdoor table, eating pizza. When I took a seat with them, they hardly spoke to me.

For the next few days, in the morning class breaks before lunchtime, they would take complicated passive-aggressive measures in an attempt to dissuade me from wanting to eat with them. The most painful of these was the time that they told me that they had invited Jason Fuller to lunch.

Everyone knew that Jason Fuller was my arch-nemesis. There were a lot of reasons why I disliked that bastard, but the most recent one was that he had snitched on me for writing graffiti. He had done this in order to claim the $100 cash reward that the school police officer had offered. The day after I got back from being suspended, Fuller had walked around with a new pair of Adidas, telling everyone that I'd bought them for him.

But this had nothing to do with Jason Fuller, really. What it boiled down to was that Andy and Tim didn't like me enough to pay an extra quarter for lunch.

(As an aside, I got a delivery job for American Pie my senior year of high school. I didn't actually need the money because I had just turned 18 and was getting my dad's social security in the form of big checks from the government every month. Andy and Tim stopped going to the pizza place altogether. After a while, I quit the job without giving any notice, and the manager told me I was "really unprofessional and gay.")

(Also, a few years later, I dated that school cop's daughter, and one night she got completely naked behind that high school and we had sex. I don't know what that means exactly, but fuck cops and fuck Jason Fuller's ugly fucking Adidas.)

High school fucking sucked.

I light my cigarette on one of the candles on the table and stand up and walk away.

The dancing starts.

I have another beer.

In the bathroom, I look at myself in a full-length mirror and feel good about my decision to wear a jacket but no tie.

I walk out and get in my van and drive back to Jasper and Kit's place. I don't want to think about how I used to be Mormon. I don't want to think about high school. I don't want to think about our wedding. I just want to hang out with my queer anarchist friends.

They are happy to see me, and we are cozy in the front room of their house. I get the bottle of wine that I had planned on drinking with the Tempe zinester woman out of the van. Easy climbs in my lap. We watch TV.

Trains must go by in the night, but I don't wake up.

I have a hard time getting out of bed because I don't have enough money left for a breakfast burrito. This is the day I have been planning on driving home, but you two and the dog are still in Taos, so I ask Kit and Jasper if they mind if I stay another day.

Kit chants, "Move in! Move in! Move in!" and I blush.

I smoke the last of my American Spirits and find enough change scattered around the van to afford a pack of Pyramid Blues.

Jasper goes to work, so Kit and Hunter and I sit on the front porch and smoke and drink coffee and watch the trains go by. Kit and I talk while Hunter listens.

We talk about hierarchal polyamory versus non-hierarchal polyamory. Kit grew up Mormon too. They are a descendant of Parley P. Pratt. Mitt Romney is their third cousin or something. They say that when they told their mom that were polyamorous, their mom said, "so you're going back to your

Mormon roots, huh?'

I say, "I don't want to go back to the cold in New Mexico. I just want to stay in Tucson all winter."

"Do it."

"I will seriously consider it."

I read Jasper's poetry manuscript. It's really fucking good.

Jasper gets back from work, and then at some point it gets dark.

Hunter has the disheveled, tuned-in, dropped-out look of an amateur psychonaut, so I ask where I can find some San Pedro cactus.

He says, "It's growing all over the place, man."

"Yeah, yeah, but where?"

So we put on our shoes and go for a walk. First we walk to a closed law office and cut about two doses worth. Then a planter box on the sidewalk in front of a bar downtown, and then a huge hedge of it that surrounds a house that looks like Diego Rivera might live in it.

We are walking home and I know it's back to New Mexico in the morning. I am a coatimundi for having lived so many lifetimes. I am a kit fox for feeling like I am torn between so many homes, so many different deserts. I am a ring-tailed cat, always feeling at least low-level nervousness and fuckedupness. I used to think I was some sort of holy man, but no longer.

I haven't taken mescaline since 2014, actually, but I know that you like it. I like it too, but I can't handle the taste anymore. It makes me puke long before I'm supposed to.

The last time I did mescaline was with you and him both. I wandered through the woods and wept when I saw a deer. He cut stigmata into the back of his hands with a sharp rock.

The last drug I did was in August of 2015, and it was meth. That was with both of you too. We thought it was MDMA, but it was meth.

The last time you two did mescaline was a couple weeks ago. You wandered into the woods by our house and drank the green goo, and you fucked, and the condom broke.

I'm bringing you some more mescaline though. I want to supportive and thoughtful. I want to believe.

The next morning I hug them all and tell them to come visit New Mexico. My gas tank is maybe half-full, so I drive east on I-10 and find a busy truck stop where I can gas-jug. The first person I walk up to gives me a ten-dollar bill.

The second person I walk up to agrees to put some gas in my jug, but then the first guy comes over and says, "Hey buddy, I just gave that asshole ten dollars!" He leaves.

"Is that true?" the second guy asks me.

"Yeah, but I've got to get all the way to Albuquerque. I mean, I really appreciate that he gave me money, but even if I fill my tank all the way up, I'm going to have to do this again before I get home."

The second guy says, "Yeah, I know where Albuquerque is," and gives me five gallons.

The third person I talk to, this super beautiful woman, agrees too.

I say, "So, are you from around here?"

"I'm from Mexico, but I live in Tucson, yeah."

"Where in Mexico?"

"Hermosillo."

"I've been to Hermosillo," I say. "It's a great city."

She looks incredulous, probably because she doubts that anyone who had actually been to Hermosillo would describe it as "great."

"Yeah," I say. "I went down there a couple years ago and then over to Kino. I love the state of Sonora."

Now she believes me.

That was another time that I was traveling broke, but the memories are all good. You and I set up our tent on the porch of an empty vacation rental house and watched whales for three days. We drank mescal and ate ramen and tortillas.

The beautiful woman is filling up my gas jug when one of the truck stop employees approaches.

The employee says, "Is he bothering you, ma'am?"

"No, no. Not at all."

Damn fucking straight, I think.

The employee says, "Well, we got some complaints that people were out here bothering people and asking for things, so I just wanted to make sure everything was good."

I thank the employee, and she leaves.

The beautiful woman from Hermosillo gives me five gallons.

I'm pouring it into my tank, spilling gas all over myself. A redneck-looking lady at another pump calls over to me.

She says, "Come see me when you're done there. I have, like, six dollars on the pump that didn't go in."

Then the manager of the Truck Stop walks up to my van.

He says, "We can't have you out here doing this. You can finish pouring that in, and then you have to leave."

"That lady was going to give me some already. Can I still get that from her?"

"You can finish pouring that in, and then you have to leave."

"Okay. Thank you."

When he leaves, the redneck lady comes over to the van and puts some cash in my hand.

"They can't stop me from giving you this. I'll just go get my change inside."

I feel like people are mostly good, except when they are being paid to be dicks. Driving out of the truck stop parking lot is the last time that I will feel this optimistic about humanity.

I drive to another truck stop and get my tank topped off. With the cash, I buy another pack of cigarettes and a Godfather's personal pizza.

Driving on I-10 East, I think about how some men will drive around with their wives or girlfriends naked in the passenger seat of their cars so that other people on the road will get a peek. These men are called candaulists, named after King Candaules of the ancient kingdom of Lydia who came up with an elaborate plan so that his bodyguard, Gyges, would see his wife, the queen, as she was undressing. The name Candaules apparently means "dog throttler." I drive slowly and look over at every car that passes. All bullshit.

I open my laptop on the passenger seat and put on some more of the porn that I downloaded in the Chandler Starbucks. The van is higher than most other vehicles on the highway, but every time a semi truck passes me, I close my computer so the driver won't see. I don't dare do any dog throttling, and after a while I get bored and start listening to podcasts.

When I cross the state line, the sun is still up, but it's

setting by the time I reach Deming. I cut northeast from there to avoid Las Cruces. The short section from there to the spot near Hatch where I pop out onto the I-25 is so breathtaking that I make a vow never to try to describe it to anyone who hasn't driven it.

Now the sun is down, and I turn on the radio. I was hoping that I would have found some hitchhikers by now, but at least the noise from the radio helps keep me from being lonely. This is Tuesday, November 8th, 2016, the night of the presidential election. Things are looking bleak. As a prison abolitionist, I don't agree with the rhetoric of "Hillary for Prison," but I didn't vote for her either. I didn't vote for anyone. Maybe I should have. I listen. I worry. Then New Mexico turns blue and I feel shitty for thinking my guilt is somehow absolved.

If voting changed anything, blah, blah, blah. On the other hand, if *not* voting changed anything then they'd make *that* illegal too.

New Mexico. I'm a roadrunner for being in love. Driving faster miles an hour. I'm in love with modern moonlight. Into the South Valley, then ABQ and east on I-40 toward Tijeras. By the time I get home, an overt fascist is the president elect of the United States of America.

I recently did a tarot reading for myself. The card that represented me as the querent was the reversed emperor.

You are a red-tailed hawk for loving me, for being with me. You are the ball of jumping cholla spikes that gets stuck in my calf for telling him "I love you."

I don't know what he is for loving you. I never knew before either, though.

I don't know whether or not I believe in tarot, but I know

that I definitely don't believe in myself.

I am that buzz that people would hear and the charge that they would feel on their skin if it wasn't already too late. I am the electric hum after the end of the world for loving both of you.

Los Huevos del Señor

I wanted to get hit by a car.

I'd heard about drunk, suicidal types running out onto the freeway and putting their heads through some poor, unsuspecting bastard's windshield, turning their bones to powder against the hood in a gory scene of unholy carnage. That wasn't for me. My plan was to casually step off the curb and get clipped by a passing Fiat Uno, or some other equally common, equally small, relatively powerless vehicle. No head injuries. No broken back. All I wanted was a fractured arm or leg or collar bone: just enough to get me sent back home to Utah, but not enough to be permanently crippling.

For weeks, as I walked through the neighborhood on the north end of Montevideo where I had been stationed for the past month or so, I eyed every car that passed, gauging its speed, mentally measuring the height of their bumpers and hood, the thickness of its windshield. It would look like an accident. That was certain. I would appear careless or stupid, anything but deliberate.

My companion, a fellow white shirt-, tie-, and backpack-wearing Mormon missionary, had no idea what I was up to. He was Elder George Tree hailing from Texas City, Texas, and he was pious as hell. Or at least that's what he—along with the rest of the battalion of clean-cut Christers and secret raging masturbators serving their two years in Uruguay—wanted everyone to think. He had always been an active Mormon, had never dated girls who wore two-piece bathing suits and was much more thoughtful and kind to his widowed mother than I was to mine. He was unbearably nerdy, talking endlessly of fantasy novels and sneezing in these magnificent eruptions of snot that actually lifted his feet off the ground. We had spent a painful month together, trying to convert heathens and meanwhile keep each other entertained with everything we had ever done, all the stories we knew, the gross stuff we could do with our eyelids. We were like prison cellmates, cut off from the world, rotting away together. He was stiff and boring, and I hated him.

One night, as we returned to our tiny apartment after a particularly unsuccessful day that had been spent knocking on doors and trying to convince total strangers to let two weirdo foreign religious fanatics into their houses so they could share some good news, the word, the holy gospel of Christ according to the Church of Jesus Christ of Latter Day Saints, I spotted a poster stapled to a light post.

"Elder," I said, "there's a free reggae concert in *la Plaza*

Colón." I looked closer. "And it's tonight. We should go." I knew his response before he even looked at me.

"No way. You know that's against the rules. We have to be obedient, Elder."

"We should just walk through the park and check it out," I said. He didn't say anything, but rather kept walking toward the house, refusing to make my requested detour.

Obedience. Fucking obedience. The concept was drilled into every poor missionary's head at every possible opportunity. If you aren't obedient then the Holy Ghost won't want to be with you, our leaders told us. And without the Power of the Holy Ghost nobody will feel the truth of your words, they said. And if nobody feels the truth of your words and gets baptized then your two years will have been a waste. Make the most of your time working for The Lord! Onward Christian soldiers!

And it wasn't just the Ten Commandments we had to abide by, either. You know, "Thou shalt not kill," et cetera. There was a little white book filled with rules that all missionaries carried around with them in their shirt pockets. The list was huge, monumental. No chewing gum in public. Wake up at six-thirty. Go to bed at ten-thirty. No caffeinated drinks. No keeping pets. No reading of any book that isn't one of the six preapproved books on this list. No music other than hymns or classical. Missionaries may e-mail their families only once a week and have no more than thirty minutes to do so. Missionaries may call home twice a year, at Christmas and on Mother's Day, but only one hour of conversation will be permitted. No sex, not even kissing or holding hands. And the reason I couldn't just ditch my self-righteous moral bodyguard: every missionary must stay with his companion at all times. You know, unless one of you is in the bathroom or the shower, but don't even think about going across the street to buy some milk and Oreos without tying your tie and bringing along the ball and chain who dresses exactly like you.

This is why kids on the street with bleached hair and BMX bikes and tinny cumbia music playing on their cell phones called us *huevos*. Eggs, Spanish slang for testicles. "Because you look the same, and you're always right next to each other, *huevos*."

From the outside, it would seem simple to say, "Nuts to that, I'm going up to the park by myself, goddammit," but it was hardly that easy. Staying with your companion is the cardinal rule of Mormon missionary work. Failure to comply would result in disciplinary action: unpleasant interviews and long talks with the mission president, an older, financially stable Mormon man who is in charge of all the young missionaries in a given region. He would assign you stricter companions in the future, stripping you of all possible freedom and assuring tighter supervision. Leaving Elder Tree to walk up to the park and listen to some reggae, even for five or ten minutes, was not an option.

So I went home, telling myself that the music probably wasn't that good. I probably wasn't missing anything. I loosened my tie and sat down at my desk to plan the following day's activities (knock on doors, talk to people who were too busy dealing with the intricacies of normal life to care about some Son of God who may or may not have lived and died over two thousand years ago) and let the evening breeze cool me down after a day of schlepping around in the hot sun. If I listened carefully, I could hear the bass floating over from the park, through the trees, over the railroad tracks, and into the open window. Somebody was playing an up-tempo version of "Long Shot Kick de Bucket" by the Pioneers, and I tapped my fingers. George Tree, that long, tall, greasy son of a bitch, stood up and closed the window.

Six hundred and one more days. I sighed.

It wasn't just the long list of rules or the repressed nutjob asshole fellow missionaries that were getting me down. What was really rotting inside my brain were all the things that I had been learning about The Church that the ever-energetic legion of Sunday school teachers had forgotten to mention. The whole organization, even from its very inception, is plagued with a history of racism, sexism, bigamy, controversy, perversity, plagiarism, science fiction, bizarre invention, censorship, violence, and blackmail. Another missionary stationed close by had recently informed me, to my great alarm, that the Mormon temple ceremony, something that a long line of church youth leaders, bishops, and family members had told me was sacred and important—*the most important thing in the whole world*—was directly ripped off from the Freemasons. The secret handshakes, the costumes, the altar, all of it. The more I learned, the less I bought into it, and the worse I felt about sharing the message that I was supposed to. Some of the people I talked to actually gleaned hope from it, clinging on like everything depended on it. I had headaches during the day and couldn't sleep at night.

While desperately trying to define my belief—or lack thereof—I had been reading canonical books of Mormon scripture that, until recently, I had never been interested enough in to decipher and charge through. There were parts where the Lord had supposedly revealed, through the prophet Joseph Smith of course, that Smith's first wife, Emma, needed to be subservient and supportive of him, that she needed to be accepting of his other wives. There was Paul, of New Testament fame, who wrote things like "let your women keep silence in the churches." There were pages and pages detailing punishments and curses for a myriad of garden-variety sins and offenses. In the morning I pored over the scriptures and their bizarre contents, and in the afternoon I trekked door to door telling people that God was our Heavenly Father who loved all of his children equally. As instructed, I told them that He wanted us to be happy. He wanted the very best for us, and the only thing that we, as his beloved children, had to do was to obey his commandments, go to his churches, pay tithes, and stop doing a bunch of stuff that we liked, stuff that felt *good*.

I wanted to go home, but it wasn't that simple. Where I came from, serving a mission was a matter of honor. I had family members and friends who were praying for my well-being, thanking God for the work I was doing, using my decision to serve as a good example for their younger children. They believed there was an actual war between good and evil, between God and Satan, and that I was on the front lines. They were counting on me, and while my faith was bloodied and slowly dying, theirs was still strong, and who the fuck was I to take that away? Who was I to sow doubt, to disappoint, to defect? So instead of going AWOL I opted to get injured, to limp home with a purple heart.

As Elder Tree and I walked through the park the next

morning, stepping over cigarette butts and plastic cups and watching workers break down the stage, I just couldn't handle it anymore. Bruce Banner's skin turns green when he feels the frustration, anger, and desperate dismay that I felt then. Like Samson, he rips his clothes and starts smashing shit, beating people's brains in and howling. All I did was step off the curb and into the street.

I didn't even look at the little blue Peugeot as it whipped around the corner, past the bakery and right at me. I knew it was there. The shrill shout of squealing brakes told me, as did my companion, who shouted, "Elder, look out!" I closed my eyes and waited for the impact.

When I opened them a moment later I was still standing, uninjured. I was still in north Montevideo, still wearing my nametag and tie, and the driver of the Peugeot was leaning out the window, sweating and screaming at me.

"Estás loco, muchacho?" Are you crazy?

I waved and stepped back onto the curb.

Work of Serious Literary Merit

Braden and I were to the part of the tour in which we were really annoyed with each other. A week and a half in. Our third to last show was in Oakland, a town in which Braden knew everybody and I knew nobody. So while he caught up with friends before the show I walked around and smoked cigarettes and lusted after the millions of pretty punk girls I saw.

What a place, I thought.

But where some people see some kind of beauty others see the symptoms of an unmistakable disease.

Old black people in the streets saw me as what I was, another white punk currently geographically positioned in Oakland, just like thousands of other white punks, and they shook their heads at me. I couldn't blame them.

I walked back to the house where the show was. I set up my merch, then sat on the porch and smoked cigarettes and drank Twisted Tea and kept to myself.

People came to the show. Local acts set up and played.

I felt lonely and far from everything.

People were at the show to see music performances, not to listen to me read short stories.

I was doing nothing good for anyone by being in this town.

I opened another Twisted Tea.

Lit another cigarette.

I wasn't even doing anything good for myself.

A punk girl came out of the house and sat next to me and bummed a smoke. Her name was Mia. She was studying literature at Berkeley and she was very beautiful. We talked about the tour so far and about my writing. She said she was excited to hear it. She put her hand on my leg as she said this. Then it was time for me to read.

I told myself I wasn't going to chicken out. I was going to ask her out after the show.

I stood up in front of the gathered crowd with a microphone and a stack of my zines.

Just trick them into thinking that you are capable and confident and not as drunk as you are.

Mia sat in the very front of the crowd. Crossed legs on the floor.

I started to read my opener story, one that would sort of break the ice before I got into my usual sad boy bullshit.

People were laughing. They were smiling at me and nodding their heads and having a good time.

My eyes went around the room.

Braden looked like he liked me.

His cool friends had expressions of enjoyment.

Man, it felt great.

I looked at Mia.

She was not smiling or laughing. She looked fucking disgusted, the same look someone has when they find maggots in their kitchen trash after getting back from vacation.

As soon as I finished that first story, she stood up and left the party. She didn't even get to hear my serious Literary work about driving drunk or being sad about my exes.

I did not go out on a date with anyone that night.

A few nights later, after we had done a show in Seattle, it was the last stop of our tour. A stoner kid party in Caldwell, Idaho. Caldwell is outside of Boise, and there really wasn't much to it. Just a bunch of redneck kids drinking beer and smoking bongs in a low-ceilinged basement.

I thought to myself, Just trick them into thinking that you are capable and confident and not as drunk as you are.

They seemed pretty disinterested in my stories.

They were pretty disinterested in Braden's music too. They wanted to hang out and talk and get fucked up. I couldn't blame them.

I went and smoked a cigarette in the front yard and looked up at the moon and thought about going home.

"Hey man," said someone in a voice with a thick country accent.

I turned around, and there was this kid from the show who'd come up to shake my hand. A big old cowboy in a NASCAR ball cap, vest, wranglers, and shitkicker boots. He looked cool as hell. He introduced himself. He absolutely was not getting a degree in literature. He worked on his family's pig farm.

He said, "Brother, I really enjoyed your first story. It made me think. What makes Ms. Pac Man a woman anyway? Hell, what even makes me a man?"

I smiled, and I thought, "I did it."

Are you a beautiful literature major or are you an Idaho pig farmer?

I only ask because now I will tell you the story that I told to both of them.

Ms. Pac Man

Ms. Pac Man is no more than a blob, a bright yellow circle with a pink bow on the top of her head. She moves through a maze, alternately chasing or being chased by ghosts and eating things that she happens upon.

But everyone knows how to play Ms. Pac Man.

There is a Ms. Pac Man arcade machine in the pizza place I go to almost every day. The art on the outside of the machine sexualizes that spherical sweetheart in a way that the game's primitive graphics cannot: supple lips and thin arms and long legs that must have *something* between them. No boobs though, no mammaries. Is she not a mammal? How does that bow stay on her head if she doesn't have any hair?

The question is then, is Ms. Pac Man a reptile?

Or maybe: would you still fuck Ms. Pac Man if she were

a reptile?

Consider other folks that you do fuck or often think about fucking. Would you have sex with your husband if he were a lizard? What about the short blond girl with all the tattoos who works at the pizza place and won't ever give you her real phone number?

Surely there are people who won't fuck non-reptiles. If you can think of it, somebody, somewhere, is into it. These folks meet each other through online message boards where they trade fantasies of komodo dragons and the "ultimate" crocodile. Then, one lady posts that video of a woman pushing a thousand baby eels out of her anus, and people freak out big time.

"wtf eels arent even reptiles."

And, "Take a fucking biology class, you perverted bitch."

Of course, it's especially hard to be attracted to Ms. Pac Man when her exact physical dimensions are so unclear. Like, is she bigger or smaller than a breadbox? Maybe she's only marble-sized, in which case she could enter your body through your butthole and navigate the complex maze that are you guts, alternately chasing and being chased by ghosts.

An Unfolding

It was late afternoon, and the crowd of students was finally waning. I sat on a cement bench, my boots crossed in front of me, heels on cooling dirt rubbed raw of grass and packed concrete-hard. Around me were university buildings, rigid, and around those sat the rest of a smoggy city on the westernmost perch of the Rockies. It was the spot where the stylish Japanese students stood and dropped the butts of expensive cigarettes. The sun shone sideways over the desert, broke through the blue spruce and onto my face.

Martín found me on this existential pinhead and slapped me on the shoulder, startling me upright. I stood, and we embraced and began walking downhill toward the corner where the light rail stops on its way downtown.

"How have you been, brother?" he asked, and I started

in, talking and not letting up, catching breaths quickly and going on. I told him of the girls I had been seeing and of the guy I had met the weekend before, a black-clad and somber punk that I picked up at a show at the collective, about how I left a backpack full of library books in his bedroom and was too embarrassed to go back and retrieve them. I talked about anarchist theory, about its inevitable acceptance by the masses. This led to stories about the bikes I was building and of the skateboard tricks I had been learning. I told him a little bit about my art, but not too much.

He didn't speak, but smoked, listening. Each time I said something that interested him, he turned, his hair brushing across his shoulders, to look at me with his good eye. He was blind in his left, a blunt, watery-gray mass of dead tissue that made people uncomfortable to look into. He refused to cover it up with a patch, or even with sunglasses. Instead, he let it float free through this world like a broken spell, something turned over to violence and harshness, a ghost in his socket.

Martín hadn't always been blind, of course. The eye had been penetrated on two occasions. The first time was when we were children. Martín's mother had spent her whole life gardening, and a surreal jungle overtook the lot on which her house sat, thick and dark and wetted by an array of sprinklers so expansive and complex that it should have been criminalized way out here in the dry West where we grew up. She had a real collection out there, specimens from Africa and the Mongolian Steppes and the Southern Cone of South America, species, entirely alien to each other in nature, which twisted and intertwined like a bizarre, half-acre wrought iron sculpture.

One gnarled bush, thick with inch-long thorns, was our castle. It had grown in such a way that there was a tunnel, just tall and wide enough for us to crawl through on our hands and knees, one behind the other. After five feet or so, the tunnel opened up into a little cave in which we could lie on our backs and look up through the branches and into the blue-white sky.

Once, lying there like that, together in this womb of flora, a rattlesnake snuck up, wriggling between us. Martín started and sat up, perfectly skewering his eyeball on a thorn that protruded from the low ceiling of the cave. He cried and the snake hurried off.

The second blow he sustained to the eye, taken in my defense, happened last year in a fight outside of a house party. The aggressor, a muscled and tightly-wound straight-edger, had just come upon conclusive evidence that I had been having ill-advised sexual interaction with his fiancé. He pushed me backwards off the porch and leapt down upon me, landing a few solid punches to the head before Martín pulled him off. Another of the straight-edger's crew picked up my beer bottle, which I had let fall onto the lawn, and shattered it into Martín's face. He dropped to the ground next to me. Our faces were inches apart, our injuries tributaries to a common shallow puddle of spilled blood that grew between us on the sidewalk.

The straight-edger and his crew delivered a few well-placed kicks each and took off. An hour later, an emergency room doctor removed a shard of glass the size of my thumbnail from my friend's already dead eye.

I kept talking, and it wasn't until we cut through the empty stadium parking lot that I was finally interrupted. A black car pulled in front of us and braked. The passenger window rolled down, and a girl, magazine-blonde, leaned out.

"Hey," she said. "Um. Do you guys have a smoke I could bum?"

Martín took his pack from his pocket and shook out a cigarette and handed it to her. She took it and turned in her seat to listen to something that someone in the back was saying. She faced us again.

"If you give me three more I'll show you my tits."

"Deal," I said, though neither the cigarettes nor the tits belonged to me. I grinned at the ridiculousness of it.

She began lifting up her shirt, ready to unfold herself to us. Martín stopped her.

"Please," he said, holding up his hands. She held her shirt halfway up her stomach, waiting. "I'm not going to give you anymore cigarettes. I can see boobs on the Internet."

He sidestepped the car and began to walk toward the train stop. I looked at him and then at the moment lost and then hurried to catch up.

"If anarchism ever gets accepted by the masses," he said, "then I'll become a communist dictator or a CEO or some kind of priest. I'll run in the complete opposite direction. They're always wrong, the masses," he said. He smiled, and the sun caught in his bad eye and stuck there, twinkling. For a moment, he looked as though he were joking.

Sex Spell for Raven

I told Raven how excited I was that Ruby was moving to New Mexico. I thought it was fate maybe. At one time in the past, I felt like I was in love with Ruby, and I told Raven about how I might see Ruby again because she was going to move to Taos. I have a picture somewhere on my hard drive of Ruby standing in a river, bending over to look at a rock. She is wearing a light summer dress.

I even wrote a story about Ruby once. It was mostly about how my two friends were being competitive with each other in their separate attempts to fuck her one time on the Fourth of July a few years ago.

Neither of them managed such a thing.

Although in real life David did pull me aside and ask for a condom. I gave him one even though I knew he wasn't going to get the chance to use it. I left that part out of the story.

I've told Raven about Dave too. Not the big things about him, but the things that are easy to talk about, like skateboarding, and taking mescaline together, and the time a couple weeks ago when he got drunk and tried to shoot me with a bb gun because I was wearing Carhartts, and he thought they would protect me from the sting, but he missed and hit Atalanta in the ass cheek in her little shorts.

Atalanta took it pretty well. She just rolled her eyes all the way out of her head.

It's never really happened the other way around. I haven't talked about Raven to Ruby or Dave or Atalanta. It's not because I have better things to talk about with these people. It's not even because Raven and I have never been in a river together, or because Raven has never tried to shoot me just because I was wearing Carhartts.

I don't talk to these people about Raven because I don't want to jinx it. Even writing this right here might jinx it.

That's what I'm worried about.

This spell isn't the kind of spell where you write out what you want to have happen.

This is the kind of spell where you just set your intention and know that it probably won't happen. But if it does, and it could maybe, then the spell worked.

We are Both Hungry Tigers

I didn't know Alejandro before I stayed at his house, but because he was Brad's friend I felt like I did. Brad talked about him all the damn time. They were like brothers.

I was traveling around, aimless and nearly destitute, about to pass through Portland, and I needed a safe place to park my van for a couple nights. By that point I had worn out my welcome in a lot of places, so I sent Alejandro an email.

I said, "I know it's short notice so if it doesn't work out no worries it's okay."

He wrote back and said, "Tomorrow is great." And he gave me his address.

The next day I drove into Portland from the south. It was rush hour, which made me start to feel the sort of craziness I had been trying to run away from in the first place, but I had no choice but to keep slowly winding my way through downtown, getting more and more anxious. Driving over the Hawthorne Bridge in my big 1991 Dodge made me feel like I had only two choices: to run headlong into oncoming traffic or else to sail off the edge and into the Willamette.

What idiot, I wondered, designed this city to sit on either side of this huge fucking river?

I made it across fine.

I kept going, and finally, after much sweating and muttering, I found Alejandro's place, and I parked. I sat for a while before getting out of the van, trying to calm myself.

I was still sitting there, staring off into nothing, when he came out of the house grinning, looking like a young Cheech Marin with his black mustache.

He stared down at me from the front porch.

"Alright, Utah license plates," he said.

He made some coffee, and we drank it. I grabbed a bottle of cheap vodka out of the van, and we drank that next. I started to feel better. For a while, we talked about Brad, about what the hell he was going to do with his life. Before it got too dark, we took Alejandro's dog for a walk down to the river where she chased a tennis ball and barked at other dogs. There were sailboats tied up to a public dock. If you lived in a van, you were considered homeless. If you lived on a sailboat, you were a captain.

We went back to the house. On the way, he bent over and picked some mint that was growing in somebody's yard. I put one of the leaves in my mouth and chewed it up. It was the best mint I'd ever tasted. It was sweet, like a mojito, like it already had lime and brown sugar in it.

He said, "There are some really great trees in this neighborhood."

We stood under a big one and chewed on pieces of mint leaves.

In the daylight, this one has so many different greens, he said.

Alejandro thought like this, in colors, or in shades of them. He had hung his own paintings all over his house, but not in a self-important way, like some people might do to remind themselves and everyone else that they were artists, that they deserved an additional measure of patience and respect. No, he probably just felt okay with who he was and what he did, despite everything about the way the world was. His paintings were good. They were big. They took up the right amount of space.

He sprayed the dog with a hose to get the river water off, and he rubbed her down with a towel. We drank more, sitting on the floor, looking at his paintings on the walls and talking again about Salt Lake City and our mutual friend.

Then I said that the last time I had been in Portland was in 2010, and I couldn't remember anything about the city because I had been so drunk and high the whole time. I told the story about passing out on the sidewalk in front of Voodoo Donuts and my friends saying, "You look too wasted, Nate. You're going to get us picked up by the cops."

He said, "Do you want to see the city?"

He asked, "Are you cool to drive right now?"

I said that after another cup of coffee I would be, so he put a pot on, and I drank as much water as I could while we were waiting for it to finish brewing. Despite all that, I was still kind of drunk when I drove downtown, but it was a weeknight, and there was little traffic on the road compared to what there had been earlier. In that moment, I remembered that I have always loved to drive drunk, to roll down the window and stomp on the gas. This series of thoughts is one that never comes to me while I am sober. My brain can only access this part of myself, the sincere enjoyment of this terrible crime, while I am already fucked up and driving.

He gave me directions, turn left, turn left again, and I parked in front of an old building.

His studio was on the sixth floor.

"This is the last building in Portland that has an elevator operator, and he goes home at four-thirty," he said.

We took the stairs.

He unlocked the studio, and we went inside.

It was a small, rundown office space, with tarps taped down over the carpets. There was oil paint all over everything and a few finished paintings hanging on the walls. He leaned forward to look at one of them and touched one corner of it very gingerly with his fingernail.

"This is going to take forever to fucking dry," he said.

He opened the window, and we went out on the fire escape and looked over downtown. It would have been the best place in the world to smoke a cigarette, but we had both quit recently and neither of us had any.

He said, "This is a good place for people watching. One day, right over there, I saw this dude punch a woman in a wheelchair in the face. But, like immediately, six big dudes jumped on him and beat the shit out of him."

There was a ladder that went from where we stood up to

the roof. I asked him if he had ever climbed it.

"I'm afraid of heights," he said.

I didn't blame him. It was rickety and sketchy, and in order to get up there, you would first have to climb over the rail of the fire escape, six stories over the street, and then sidestep your way over to the ladder. Then you could climb up.

I said, "Let's do it."

I climbed over and hung onto the rail so that my butt was out over the street. With my right hand, I carefully let go of the rail and grabbed a rung of the ladder. I eased my right foot over, then my left hand, my left foot, and then I was on the ladder.

Alejandro looked at me like I was a crazy motherfucker.

I thought, You're too wasted, Nate. You're going to get us picked up by the cops.

I climbed up the ladder and onto the roof.

I leaned over the edge and said, "You coming?"

He shook his head like he couldn't believe what the fuck he was doing, and he climbed over the rail of the fire escape. He looked at his hand, and then at the ladder, and then back at his hand. He knew that he had to let go of one piece of metal to grab hold of another one, but he couldn't make himself do it. I saw his muscles tense up.

"You alright," man?

He didn't answer.

You okay?

"I can't do it," he said. "I can't do it. I can't do it. I can't do it."

I said, "You don't have to do anything."

He was still holding onto the rail, still out over the street.

He shouted up to me, "My hands are starting to get sweaty."

I shouted, "Just climb back over."

But he was frozen.

He was too scared to climb up and too scared to go back.

He was petrified with fear.

I got back on the ladder and started climbing down again.

But now I was afraid too.

And now I could feel MY hands getting sweaty.

It was a long way down.

I climbed down until I was right next to him, both of us afraid of heights now, both of us drunk. I looked over at him. Sweat dripped through his mustache and his eyes bugged out. He looked crazy. I couldn't climb onto the fire escape until he did. The ladder was in the way. I thought about the paint slowly drying on his paintings, about the street below, about the Hawthorne Bridge, about his dog in the river, about the taste of mint leaves, about a man punching a woman in a wheelchair in the face.

Lemons

It should have been none of my business how much Chaz did or did not draw, but I couldn't let it go. It was just that he was such a damn good visual artist, and I couldn't bear to see all his talent going to waste. He was doing some illustrations for a few small magazines, comics sometimes, deeply moving black and white Southwestern landscapes. I always thought he should be doing more. For every drawing he did finish, I knew there were a hundred more that would never emerge onto the page. I don't know how he could live like that, with each of these potential masterpieces sitting heavy in his gut, wriggling around each other like water snakes in a balled up orgy.

I made it my job to pry Chaz away from the demonic distractions that perpetually overcame him: documentaries about conspiracy theories, internet porn, his bong, et cetera. I badgered him relentlessly. I tricked him into working, disguising it as hanging out. That was the main reason I invited him to get coffee with me.

We met and ordered our drinks and sat down.

"What's been happening, man?" I asked.

"Oh, not so much."

"You draw anything lately?" He stirred almond milk into his coffee and stared at me. I continued. "You still working on that comic zine?"

"Off and on. You write anything lately?"

"A few poems, some song lyrics and stuff, but I've been kind of dry on ideas, I guess."

He nodded.

"You know," I said, making a show of looking around, "this coffee shop is a pretty good atmosphere for creativity. Maybe I could get some writing done here. And you could draw. Let's do it for an hour, and then we'll share what we come up with."

He agreed but without enthusiasm. I opened a blank Word document on my laptop.

An hour later, I read him a sloppy three-page poem that I had written about some beautiful crust punk girls that had been sitting at a nearby table. I called it "look but dont touch." It was garbage.

Chaz turned his sketchbook around so that I could see it. His drawing was done in black ink and spread across two pages. It showed a brick, one-story house, which sat on a street that ran up and down a steep hill. It looked like the house was in California or at least somewhere warm. There were five or six fruit trees in the front yard. One tree was covered in lemons. There were hundreds of them, just an insane amount of lemons.

Inside the house was a young woman, maybe the same age as Chaz and me, mid-twenties, sitting at the kitchen table. She pushed around the food on her plate, but didn't really eat any of it. She was too busy thinking to be very hungry.

The young woman had grown up in a religious family and had always believed that after she and her loved ones died they would get to be together in heaven for all eternity. It was a nice thought, but when she turned 18, she went away to college and came to realize that, although she loved her family very much, their religion was kind of fucked up. Not only did her former convictions no longer resonate, they made her angry and upset. Her beliefs about heaven faded.

She didn't feel like eating because she was sad that her grandfather had died a couple weeks earlier. She remembered that when she was a child the two of them had spent an afternoon together planting that lemon tree in the front yard. Her grandpa dug the hole and got the tree in place, and she shoveled the dirt back in and watered it.

The tree grew okay, but for years and years it never gave any lemons. It just sat there, casually doing nothing.

One night – this was when the young woman was in high school – her grandfather had come home drunk. Super drunk. He managed to park his old Ford Ranchero in the driveway before stumbling up the lawn and toward the front door. Halfway there, he fell into the lemon tree. Thanks in large to the beer belly he carried around with him, the tree split in half, right down the middle. The girl ran outside and helped him stand up and get inside to bed. The next morning, she woke up early and mended the wounded tree the best she knew how, by wrapping its trunk with duct tape.

It healed, and soon the tree started giving so many lemons that nobody knew what to do with them. They were all over the lawn. The girl and her grandfather gathered them to make lemonade and lemon meringue pies. They gave away baskets of fruit to the neighbors, but the lemons kept coming.

The young woman sat at the kitchen table, pushing her food around and thinking about her grandfather and those lemons. She knew that she wouldn't see him in heaven.

That was Chaz's drawing.

The crust punk girls stood up and left the cafe.

I Can Sleep Here

We are walking to downtown from The Hill, the neighborhood where the college students live and hang out. It is afternoon. I am not a college student. I am quite drunk.

We can never seem to shut up. We are ceaselessly fascinated by each other. And, more than we want to admit, we are awfully damn fascinated by ourselves.

I am just divorced. You have just had an abortion. We both have nose rings.

We are depressed, but there is a certain romanticism to our lives, we think.

I start dating M_____, a sex worker. I date B_____, a special education teacher. You and I buy tall boys and sit in the alley behind the coffee shop, and I tell you about how immediately after B_____ and I finished having sex in her bed, her Maine Coon cat shat diarrhea all over my arm. You laugh so hard that beer comes out of your nose, and I think maybe it's you that I'm in love with.

I sleep with a barista, and I fall a little bit in love with her. I sleep with a stripper. I fall a little bit in love with her, too.

You are finishing your degree and going back home to Germany. I cry about it like an idiot baby. I paint you a picture, but I never give it to you because it is dumb and I feel dumb.

The day after you leave, I don't know what the fuck to do.

It's morning. I have work. I wait for the bus and look at the mountains. On my headphones I am listening to a Crass album that I have open in YouTube.

I look at tickets to Germany on the internet. I text you, asking if I should buy one. I do. It costs between five and six hundred dollars. You say you will keep me fed and drunk the whole time I am with you. You are a person who breaks promises all the time, but I know this is something you would never lie about.

I work. I write papers for college kids to make extra money. I put up Craigslist ads. They keep getting flagged. I put them up again.

I go swimming. On the Fourth of July, I sleep with my housemate's best friend, and I try to convince myself that the sex is better than it actually is.

We share the mattress on your floor in Berlin. I go to work with you and hang out, and you sneak me free beers. We take ecstasy at six in the morning and roll around on your floor and get in the shower together because the water feels so good.

It's dark when we wake up. We try to party again, but I

ask you what you will do if your mom dies. We sit on a curb and cry.

We eat bread and cheese and olives. We drink red wine and Sternburg Export. Some PayPal money comes through, sent by a college student I took a couple online classes for. You don't have to buy everything for me after all.

We read artsy novels out loud to each other.

We go dancing with your friends. I snort speed off my iPhone screen, and you take more MDMA. I really enjoy the music but feel intimidated by the idea of "getting into" techno, of putting in the effort to learn things about a genre of music that is almost entirely new to me.

We sleep together, but not in the way I slept with the sex worker or the special ed teacher or the barista or the stripper or my housemate's best friend. We spoon. You kick me when I snore. We talk about making a zine entitled *I Can Sleep Here.* We don't kiss. It's not that kind of thing.

When you come back to Colorado to visit, you meet me at the public tennis courts, and I give you a hard time about not emailing me more often. We smoke cigarettes. We don't cry anymore. We go out with people and buy cocaine, and I am annoyed with how much talking everyone is doing. Everyone but us. I am not talking. You are not talking. I so badly want to hear you say something, but I feel like no one in this group deserves the pleasure of hearing your voice. In general, we are much more business-like than we have ever been.

Sometimes, right when I climb into my truck, it smells like cat piss. We drive up the canyon to the nudie spot to swim in the creek. Except when we get there, we see that Henri's car is pulled off on the side of the road. We agree that we definitely cannot fucking handle that guy right now. We go further upstream, hop over a fence, avoid some fishermen, and hang our clothes on the willows.

We want the sun to come back. We shout at it.

I say, "This belly is so goddamn white!"

You say, "These tits need some vitamin D!"

That does it. The sun comes out for a second, and you face it with your arms spread. I take a picture of you from behind, but I don't tell you. We drink tall boys.

We are still interested in each other as people. You have recently cheated on your boyfriend, and my girlfriend has recently had an abortion. It sucks so much. We are much less interested in ourselves than we once were.

"I, like, don't talk anymore," you say.

I know exactly what you mean. It used to be cool to discuss things, work things out. Communism, sexuality, polyamory, consciousness, poetry, dreams. All that dumb shit.

I don't talk anymore either.

I read a book.

You bend over to look at bugs.

I pick wildflowers.

You put your shirt on. You take it off again.

I wonder if anything reminds you of me when we aren't together.

I wish we had more beer, but we are both broke and too afraid anymore to shoplift.

I don't hear from you after you go back to Germany. I just work. I go to the bookstore, communicate as little as possible with customers, buy books for myself at a steep discount, go home and put them on my shelves.

People ask me how I'm doing.

I say, "Good, man."

I say, "It's so fucking hot outside."

After work, I go to the creek to swim. Chris and Rane are there. They offer me DMT. I have never smoked DMT before, and I think, Fuck It.

Chris loads a bowl.

I hit it.

DMT smells like a sporting goods store, I think.

I watch a trout repeatedly try to jump up a small waterfall. It is such a beautiful thing to see. It occurs to me that the trout and the waterfall and the beauty exist independent of the DMT.

Simon texts me to ask what I'm doing. Lindsay texts me to tell me her plane is about to take off. My mom sends me a picture of my grandparents holding hands in Oregon. Sara texts me wondering if I've heard of some slam poet I've never heard of and don't give a shit about. My housemate texts to see if I can be home from nine to ten tomorrow to let in the person who is supposed to fix the hot water heater. Max texts me saying that he ate greasy chicken wings and has acid reflux. Someone says, "Yo." Someone asks if I can cover their shift.

And my heart. My goddamn heart doesn't work any better than it ever has.

I'm Sorry Your Boyfriend is in the Mental Hospital Again

I'm sorry your boyfriend is in the mental hospital again.

I'm sorry that he jumped out of your car.

You were slowing down to turn, and he dropped his skateboard out the window, then swung the door open and threw himself out.

You were still going 20 miles per hour.

I don't know how his landing was, but that's where I found him.

I was on my way back from the Mexican grocery store, and he was miles from home, limping along with the bill of his hat turned up.

He had his skateboard under one arm and a garbage bag full of laundry under the other.

I offered him a ride.

He said, "I think I'd better walk."

It seems like most people stopped offering him rides after he
stole his roommate's car, and the two of them screamed at
each other like the men do who stand all night outside the
chain-link fence of the homeless shelter downtown.

I'm sorry that he ate four hits of acid while he was in that state.

He said he couldn't even feel it.

He said the same thing that time he ate those mushrooms and
fell asleep on the sidewalk in front of the 7-Eleven by the
baseball stadium.

He was slumped against the Redbox, and a man woke him up
and handed him a dollar and said, "It's getting late. Why
don't you find yourself a ride?"

Your boyfriend took the dollar.

He walked home and watched *The Warriors* on Netflix and
smoked a spliff.

The last time I ever smoked pot was with your boyfriend,
before he was your boyfriend.

That was after he got out of the mental hospital the first time.

He was feeling better, he thought.

He was flying into Salt Lake City, and could he stay at my
house for a few days?

On my icy front steps, he smoked two Marlboro Red 100s at
once, and later I had a panic attack and sat in the shower
and cried until someone brought be a Klonopin.

I'm sorry your boyfriend left his unsigned divorce papers at
your house for months.

I'm sorry you have to see the scars on his chest where he carved
"FUCK" with an old boy scout pocketknife.

I'm sorry that his family wants to send him to live with his
sister in Arizona.

I'm sorry that his dad doesn't get it.

That his sister can be a real cunt.

That he might have to start all over again.

That he will be in the place where everything went wrong,
where he learned he hated teaching high school, where he
smoked gas station spice and felt so alone.

Where his wife felt so alone.

Where he will be alone again.

Only the saguaro and coatimundi to keep him company.

I'm so sorry that your boyfriend is in the mental hospital again.

The Last Time I Almost Had a Threesome

If I had been in my apartment instead of a hospital bed, it might have been the ideal afternoon. My mind and body were braided with painkillers, and Stanley Kubrick's Eyes Wide Shut was about a thirty seconds away from the best scene of the movie. Tom Cruise gave the password, donned his robe and exquisite mask, and wandered into the great meeting hall where the creepy sex cult was getting their ritual started. I swear one of the girls on screen looked just like this girl I slept with in Las Cruces once. I couldn't see her face because she was wearing a mask too, obviously, but it looked just like her body. It might have actually been her. I mean, I can't be sure, but I'd recognize those boobs anywhere.

There's that part where the priest is chanting and waving incense around, and all the naked girls are kissing each other, and the camera follows them in one, long, circular shot. That scene, without question, is one of the most impacting moments in American cinematic history, but when the nurse walked in and saw what was on my TV screen, she just looked at me like I was a pervert or something.

"How are you doing, Mark? Feeling alright?"

"This morphine is great. Got anything to balance it out a little? A little cocaine maybe?" It was supposed to be a joke, but I'm not going to pretend to hate cocaine.

"I'll bring you some coffee," she said. "Anything else?"

For a second I thought that by "anything else" she meant "sex," and I smiled. She didn't smile back. Instead, she tightened her lips and waited, watching me. Her eyes were fixed lower than I hoped they would be. I followed them to the swaths of bandages at the end of my right leg, and was reminded of just why exactly I was in the hospital in the first place.

"No, nothing else, thanks," I said.

"How's the foot?" she asked.

I told her it was fine, just fine, and she left to fetch me some coffee. In fact, my foot was far from fine. Just a few hours earlier most of it had been amputated. It had been sawed off about halfway up, leaving a weird, toeless club.

I told myself it wasn't the end of the world. It wasn't. It's not like I had a big athletic career ahead of me or anything. And besides, having this amputated foot was already sort of starting to add to the persona I liked to think that I've cultivated for myself. It made me more mysterious, more cool. By itself, an amputation isn't nearly enough to make you cool. My mom's neighbor was a diabetic who had had both of her feet cut off. She wore pink muumuus and watered the lawn from her wheelchair. She was anything but cool. No, I was already one of those cool guys you see in bars and record stores, and my newfound status as an amputee made me more of an interesting character in the way that a half-crazy ex-marine is one. It sort of matched my dreadlocks.

This was another story to tell around the campfire or at parties. I could pull it out of my bag along with the one about how I got stabbed by a member of the Bandidos MC. Before, I was the guy who had traveled through Central America off the beaten path, from village to village, sleeping with girls who only spoke Nahuatl or Mixteco, the prettiest girls in the tribe, or whatever. Now I'm the guy who did all that shit, and has an amputated foot to boot. To boot. See what I did there?

Acting cool is a simple trick that you either figure out somewhere along the line or you don't. I'll clue you in. All you have to do is act unimpressed by anything that comes up, like you've done and seen it all before. Stay calm and uninterested, even if it *isn't* your millionth time buying mescaline from a guy with face tattoos. Do wild shit, and keep yourself from grinning. Pluck butts from the ashtray in front of the 7-Eleven and smoke them shits like they were Cuban cigars. Hell, if someone offers you a Cuban cigar, smoke it like it was a butt from an ashtray. That's how everybody knows you mean business. If you don't look cool, then you get stuck hanging out with pubey-bearded guys who think they're wizards, guys whose favorite color is "transparent."

Of course, there are a few situations in which that strategy doesn't work, when you're better off just shutting up and listening. Like with these crust punk girls, Lucy and

Rat, fellow travelers that I met at a house party in Oakland. I was being pretty funny, and we had been drinking a lot of cinnamon whiskey. Also, I had a hotel room in town, and they wanted to come back to it with me. Rat was considerably better looking than Lucy. Her body was all lean and tight under her black Flux of Pink Indians t-shirt, and Lucy's t-shirt was a little too lean and tight over her body, if you know what I mean. I didn't mind though. It was sort of a twofer-one type of a deal, and I hadn't had one of those in a couple of months. Convenient enough, right? Listen though, I don't usually stay in hotel rooms. I mean, look at me. That's obviously not my style. When I travel I'd rather couch surf or sleep under the stars or in a hostel, but I had had a long day hitchhiking, and I thought I'd reward myself with a soft bed and some internet access courtesy of La Quinta.

Anyway, what matters is that these two girls wanted to come back to my hotel. We took the bus there and snuck in the side door and crept up to my room.

"Jesus Christ, Mark," said Lucy, "how many stairs do we have to climb?"

"Quiet. I don't want to get kicked out. I'm not supposed to bring anyone here."

"Oh, what are they going to do?"

"I've only paid for one person."

"Don't be such a pussy," said Rat, and she yanked on one of my dreads pretty good.

"Why couldn't we've taken the fucking elevator?" Lucy was yelling now. I winced, pulled the keycard out of my wallet and hurried them into my room.

"Nice pad, dude," said Rat. She clicked on the TV.

"Sure beats the squat," added Lucy, looking around. "Can we order room service?"

I sat on the bed and pulled off my boots. Lucy was hefting my backpack.

"Is this yours, Mister North Face?"

"Uh, yes."

"Looks like it hasn't seen much travel."

"It's new. I stole it from REI."

Rat giggled, and then got serious.

"Where are those boomers you promised us, Mister North Face?"

I retrieved the bag of high-grade mushrooms from the side pocket of my pack and dangled it in front of the girls like a hypnotist's watch.

And we did those mushrooms in room 313 of the Oakland La Quinta, and we talked about death and anarchism and achieving immortality by uploading your brain to a supercomputer. The girls took a shower. I wasn't invited. They peeled off black jeans and t-shirts and left them in a filthy heap in front of the bathroom door. I could tell they wanted to make it happen, some sexy time. We would have once they got cleaned up, I'm sure, but by the time they stepped out of the shower I was too far gone. I know how this sounds, but I felt like I was *inside* of the carpet. I fell asleep there on the floor, while they spooned under my hard-earned hotel sheets, two crusties scrubbed clean, naked save for their wobbly, handpicked tattoos. There was tomorrow night for threesomes.

The next day we smoked a spliff and I checked out of the hotel while Rat and Lucy snuck out the back door. We ducked into Denny's for a hangover pancake brunch, and they asked if I'd ever ridden freight before.

"Sure," I said. "I'm a regular Alexander Supertramp."

"Well, we're going to catch out to Portland tonight. Want to come along?"

Threesome! I thought.

"Definitely. It's been a while since I've been through Portland."

So we headed to pick up their bags, which were made of green canvas and covered in patches and pins and grease. They looked like regular ol' turds sitting next to my North Face beauty in the back of their friend Box's pickup truck as he drove us to the train yard. Mine would get there someday.

Box hugged the girls and left, and we sat in the shade, hiding from the bull in a scratchy stand of weeds. There was nothing to do but wait. I smoked Pyramid cigarettes until my throat felt raw. I rubbed my knuckle across my gums to make sure that they weren't bleeding.

"Jesus," I said, shifting my pack to try and make it into a more comfortable pillow. "When does this train leave, anyway?"

The girls eyed me.

"I thought you said you'd ridden freight," Rat said.

"I have, I have. I've just only done it in Mexico," I said. "And Canada. Trains run on time in Canada."

To my relief, Lucy sprang to her feet.

"That's our train. Let's go!"

I grinned, thinking that I was the best sort of railroad prophet.

We hustled across the yard to a slow moving northbound

pulling empty coal cars. We jogged along parallel to it, and Rat handed her pack to Lucy and climbed onboard. She gave us a grin and a thumb up before lowering herself to the bed of the car. How the hell were we going to pee in there? I really had to go. The train was moving faster, picking up steam, as they say. Lucy threw Rat's bag first and then her own, and she too lifted herself onto the thundering, hundred shit-ton coffin. Once aboard, she hung over the top and watched me. I was sprinting now to keep up. I heaved my bag up to her like a bright blue, quick-dry football full of expensive drugs. She caught it. Rat poked her head over the side of the coal car.

"Hurry the fuck up, Mark!" she shouted.

I'm a pretty fast runner normally, but my boots crunched deep into the gravel along the side of the tracks. I groped for a hold, running my hand along the steel that was gritty with dust, finding nothing.

One of them must have shouted something, probably Lucy, because I lost focus for just one split second. And in that one split second I learned that sometimes, every once in a while, it's okay to appear curious or interested or even eager. Because worse than being uncool is watching the faces of two crust punks as they roll away to Portland while you're on your back in the Oakland gravel, covered in your own urine, and with an indiscernible mash of chewed up flesh and boot leather at the end of your right leg

Western Trash

Elder Toby wore his black Jansport-brand backpack on his front again. It looked like a fat belly. He had the zipper undone part way, and his hands were inside, fidgeting around, like always. This, along with about a million other things (his vegetarian diet, his slow manner of speaking, and the way he did his morning and night prayers sitting cross-legged on the floor instead of kneeling by his bed, just to name a few), drove Elder Wilde crazy. Elder Toby was weirder than a three-dollar bill, and that's all there was to it. And out here, in Rock Springs Wyoming, people didn't care much for weird.

"What are you doing?" Elder Wilde asked.

"What do you mean?"

"Why are you wearing your backpack like that? What are you doing in there?"

Elder Toby took his hands from his backpack and held up a string of wooden beads.

"I'm just meditating."

"What is that, a rosary? False idles, Elder!"

"Hardly. These are Buddhist prayer beads."

"The last time I checked, the plaque on your shirt had Jesus' name on it, not Buddha's."

"Buddhism is just a philosophy, Elder, not a religion. There's a lot of good we can take from it."

It was then that they reached the neighborhood they planned to spend that day knocking; a trailer park perched on the brown and dusty hill above Interstate 80, running in one direction to New York, thousands of miles further East than Elder Wilde had ever gone, and in the other direction to California, the route barely missing Farr West, Utah, his home on the range, so to speak. Elder Toby knocked on the door of one of the trailers, ending the discussion.

A woman, dressed in a faded muumuu and her hair in curlers, answered the door. She said nothing.

"Hi," said Elder Wilde. "I'm Elder Wilde, and this is my companion, Elder Toby. We're representatives of the Church of Jesus Christ of Latter-day Saints, and we're in your neighborhood today, sharing a message of Jesus Christ and his love for all of us. May we come in for a few minutes?"

The woman shut the door in their face without bothering to speak a word.

Silently, they moved on to the next trailer, then the next, and the next after that. Few people seemed to be home, and if they were, they wanted nothing from the missionaries. Elder Toby was just too bizarre for everyone. Elder Wilde had never been so sure of anything in his life. His companion was scaring people off.

"Couldn't you be more … normal?" asked Elder Wilde.

"What do you mean?"

"We're in cowboy country. Your presentation has to fit our audience if we want them to listen to us."

"But this message is for everybody."

"Just act manlier, okay? More masculine. Stand up straight. Be a preacher, not a weird mystic."

They approached a few more doors and walked away from them moments later with a familiar sense of dejection. A cold wind was blowing in from the north, bringing with it dark clouds that towered far above the surrounding mountains. The temperature dropped sharply and suddenly, and the elders could see dark torrents of rain on the horizon, streaming down from the sky like blood gushing from a wound. It didn't rain much in Rock Springs, but when it did, the sight was a brutal one. Dried-up muck and mine tailings and motor oil spewed into the infertile soil from leaking dirt-bikes and four-wheelers ran down from the hills and washed through the city streets in sludgy rivers of filth.

A dull apprehension settled over the elders as they made their way down the block. They came to a sort of run-down garage with a few big motorcycles parked out front, choppers all of them. From where they stood, Elder Wilde noted a few 1970s-era Harleys, a Triumph Bonneville, and a particularly mean-looking Honda CB 750. The building looked like it hadn't seen any business in a long time. The bay doors were shut, and from the amount of rust and water damage they had sustained they looked as if no amount of groaning and prying would see them open again. There were a few broken windows, and trash was scattered around the property. The wind picked up food wrappers and rotten plastic bags and threw them spiraling skyward. Sparse, yellow grass grew through and around old tires and neglected tools, all of which indicated that someone might just be using this godforsaken place as their home. A chain-link fence topped in barbwire surrounded the compound. The gate, which could be rolled shut and padlocked, stood just open enough for Elder Toby to squeeze through, which he did.

"Elder!" Elder Wilde called in a frantic whisper-yell. He looked over both shoulders. "What are you doing?"

"I'm going to knock. What does it look like I'm doing?"

"Are you crazy? Let's get out of here!"

"Are you scared, Elder Wilde?"

Then Elder Toby knocked loudly on the metal door of what had once been the garage's office, and Elder Wilde had no choice but to slip through the gate and join his companion. They stood there for a moment, listening to someone rustle around inside. Elder Wilde looked at the bikes. A few of them had El Salvador's blue and white flag painted on the tanks, along with some words he couldn't read. A new terror washed over him as he noticed, painted on the same part of every bike's tank, a small swastika. They must have stumbled into some sort of neo-Nazi biker commune. He was a passible Aryan, sure, and so was Elder Toby – but those prayer beads... that weird Eastern stuff... They were dead meat; he was sure of it.

Elder Wilde tried to get his companion's attention, to make a run for it, but it was then that the door cracked open.

A woman stood looking at them like in the same way she

might have if little, soft and harmless-looking, gray aliens had crash-landed their UFO outside her front door. She wore a denim vest covered in patches and pins, all of which, along with the vest itself, were stained with what looked like motor oil and some sort of flaky red-brown residue. The biggest patch was sewn across the back of the vest, a skull with a wrench in its teeth. Printed underneath in jagged letters, were the words "LAS FEMENAZIS 13."

"*Y? Que es lo que quieren?*" What do you want?

"Um," stuttered Elder Toby, "We're missionaries from the Church of Jesus Christ of Latter-day Saints. I'm Elder Toby, and this is my companion, Elder—"

"Your companion? What are you, gay? *Son maricas?*"

"No, no. On the contrary. What I mean to say is—"

"What? You have a problem with the LGBTQ+ community?"

"Not at all, not at all. We're all children of God, and that's why we're here. To share a message He has for us. May we share it with you?"

The woman looked them over carefully.

"You better not a have a problem because we're all *lesbianas* here." She swung the door open to reveal an old office, which had been turned into a sort of living room. A few women, dressed nearly identically to the first, sat on couches and watched the Simpsons, dubbed into Spanish. "*Pasen adelante.*"

The Elders went inside, and Elder Wilde whispered to Elder Toby, "Five new investigators. Jackpot."

"Here. Sit down," said one of the women, and she cleared a space off the couch by shoving a pile of backpacks onto the floor. The Elders stepped over them and sat, sinking into the ancient couch. Almost every surface of the small room was covered in identical backpacks, black JanSports, just like Elder Toby's. They all seemed to be stuffed full.

"So, do any of you believe in God?" asked Elder Wilde.

The woman who had let them in shrugged. The others didn't look away from the TV. It was as if they didn't want to acknowledge the Elders' presence.

"Well, we do," he continued. "That's why we're here. We share a message about God and his love for all of us." A groan rose from the next room, then a loud and sustained chain of violent-sounding coughs. Elder Wilde let his voice rise, speaking over the distracting noise. "We are all God's children, and he is our Heavenly Father."

The coughing stopped, and the women next the to Elders finally looked away from the TV.

Elder Wilde smiled. The word of God always prevailed.

But they weren't looking at him. They were looking at each other with nervous faces. Then they looked up at the door to the next room, which burst open loudly and suddenly Standing behind it was a woman bigger than any that Elder Wilde had ever seen. Including the thick soles of her combat boots, she must have approached seven feet. Her shoulders filled the doorway, and from them hung denim vest identical to the rest, but far more battered. Her hair was cropped short, and her boulder-sized fists were clenched. Her muscular arms were bare, covered in tattooed images of evil-looking animals and motorcycles and naked women. Elder Wilde tried to avert his eyes but he couldn't. The tattoos didn't stop where her arms met her shoulders. They continued up her throat and even onto her face. She spat on the floor.

"You *putas* think it's okay to bring THEM in here? And while I'm this hung over?"

"We thought it would be funny," said the woman who had let them in. "*Chiste.*"

"A bunch of *pallazas*, eh? Well I'm not a *pallaza*. I'm the boss around here. I'm the president of this club, and I say they get out!"

The other women stood and faced the missionaries, who sat on the couch, stiff with fear. They neared the Elders with a look of dull violence in their eyes.

"Come on, you." said one, grabbing them by their ties and hoisting them to their feet. "*La Dictadora* says we don't want to hear your sappy heavenly daddy story."

She had pulled them halfway to the door, when the leader stopped her.

"Wait." She smiled. "Yeah. I have an idea." She bent low and stuck her face close to the Elders', examining their nametags. The smell of booze and stale cigar smoke washed over them like a polluted wave. "Elder Toby, Elder Wilde, do you really love the Lord?"

"Yes."

"Yes."

"Tell me, how much do you love the Lord?"

"He is our King."

"Pretty well, anyway."

"Do you really think that we heathens need to hear the Good News?"

"More than anything," said Elder Wilde.

"Well, I'll make you a deal, Elders. You can teach us everything about God – we'll all sit down and have a nice chat.

Does that sound nice?"

They both nodded.

"Here's the condition. We'll listen to your story, IF you two kiss each other. On the lips. With plenty of tongue. You'd do that to bring a few souls unto salvation, wouldn't you? Which is the bigger sin here?"

The Elders looked at each other and then back up at *La Dictadora*.

"I think we'd better be getting on our way," said Elder Wilde.

Outside the compound, the missionaries massaged their necks, where their ties had dug into their flesh. The rain was pouring down now, but they didn't notice. They walked quickly in the direction of home. When they had gotten a few blocks away, Elder Toby swung his backpack onto his chest, as he always did, unzipped it, and reached inside for the comfort of his prayer beads. The blood drained from his face.

"Oh no."

"What? What's the matter?"

From the backpack, Elder Toby lifted a package wrapped in plastic and masking tape. It was a brick of some kind of brown powder. The backpack was stuffed full of identical bricks.

"What is that?"

"I-i-it's heroin, I think. I must have grabbed the wrong backpack when they threw us out."

"Oh no."

From behind them, over the sound of the rain, they could hear the sound of motorcycle engines roaring to life. First a couple of Harleys. Then a Triumph. Then a particularly mean-sounding Honda CB 750. They ran.

Put Me on a Dog Leash and Make Me Eat Taco Bell off the Floor

You keep thinking you will grow accustomed to a feeling of worthlessness, but you never do.

Your goal was to pay off your debt by the end of the year. Your credit card. Your overdrafted checking account. The last three thousand or so dollars of your student loans. The payments on the van you bought but that your ex-wife sold to get the money to buy herself a truck.

You are just making payments on her truck, basically.

You've been working, but you realize it isn't going to happen. This is not the year that you pay off your debt. Even on days you have off from your regular job, you go to work for your friend Gruber to make extra money.

He owns a landscaping company. You meet at his house

in the morning and go together in his truck to a client's yard, where you pull weeds.

After a while, Gruber says, "That's good enough."

He says, "That's the good thing about trying to go for a quote-unquote natural look. When I'm sick of pulling weeds, I just stop pulling weeds. It's natural."

Time for a break. You go with him to the coffee shop where he used to work before he started his own company. The baristas there are cute. They are excited to see him. When he realizes that he has forgotten his wallet, they make jokes about scanning his retinas. He giggles and puts his face over the cash register, as if it might be accepting a payment from an account linked to his eyeballs.

One of the baristas grabs the back of his head and slams his face into the cash register and laughs.

It looks like it hurt.

"Sorry," says the other barista, addressing you. "I know that seemed violent, but we all love each other. We love Gruber so much."

You can't think of anything clever to say.

You are thinking about all the times that you have wanted to grab your friend by the hair and smash his face into something, but you feel like you probably shouldn't mention that.

You pull some crumpled bills out of the pocket of your work pants and pay for the espresso.

You wish someone would grab you by the hair and smash your face into something.

You don't think you deserve it, but you've been wrong before. You probably do deserve it.

It's a safe bet.

Maybe that's how you could make some money.

Frustrated service industry workers could take out their rage and frustration by paying to let them smash your face into something.

It could be donation-based.

You don't want to be classist.

You could print up flyers and pass them out:

"Smash my face into something! Suggested donation: $5 - $10. No one will be turned away!"

Back to work, sort of. You drive with Gruber to a plant nursery almost an hour away.

On the way there, you listen to the college radio station and think about how you recently got laid.

You certainly didn't see it coming. Why would you?

So, even though you knew that you were going out on a date, you did nothing to prepare.

She came back to your house, and when you opened the door to your bedroom you said, "Sorry. It looks like a depressed person lives here."

You thought about saying something similar about your neglected, untrimmed pubic hair, but you didn't want to call any more attention to the complex ecosystem of chaos in which you seem to live.

You wonder if you are an asshole.

Probably not.

If anyone ever calls themselves and asshole, you should probably believe them.

You make a resolution to believe every self-declared asshole.

And then let them smash your face into something.

But you're not an asshole.

You're just a loser in a mountain town populated with extremely rich people.

They know some secret that you don't.

This is because you are dumb.

You and your best friends are a bunch of dumb drunks who will never pay their debts.

Like Paul, who lives out of his car.

And Jimbo, who pours shitty whiskey into a Maker's Mark bottle that he carries around in his backpack.

And Avagyan, who is dating a 21-year old.

Though, when you think about it, dating a 21-year old actually doesn't seem like such a loser thing to do.

Seems pretty cool.

This creepy guy at some hot springs once told you, "You're only as old as the woman you're holding."

You imagine dating a 97-year old woman.

About letting her smash your face into the hood of a Lincoln Continental.

About fading into the sweet peaceful caress of the universal void together.

No, you're not a loser, you decide.

And neither are any of your friends.

How could you think such horrible things about your *best* friends?

You dumb dick.

You asshole.

You really do deserve to have your face smashed into something.

And you'll get rich from it.
You'll finally pay off your ex-wife's truck.

Log

Ruby watched with some pleasure as Jonathan and Arturo, both of whom she had just met, competed for her attention.

The party was spread across someone's front lawn, and people were divided into groups, passing around bottles of wine or rum and smoking cigarettes. One group was trying to remember all the words to "Yellow Rose of Texas."

"I think they sing about 'darkies' in it," somebody said. "In the original version."

Another group, divided between those who identified as anarchists and those who identified as socialists, argued about politics. As tempers heated, they stopped passing the booze around. Those who had bottles held onto them. Those who did not started to get cranky.

Ruby and Jonathan and Arturo were a group of their own, the two of them facing her and talking. She was aware that they were attempting to "cock block" each other and imagined them as characters in a fighting videogame, like Street Fighter 2, punching and kicking wildly, competing by using the button-mashing technique, occasionally and accidentally hitting a combo. They might look for a moment like they knew what they were doing, but then they resumed their bumbling display.

She imagined that they both used similar techniques in bed, blindly stroking and rubbing and poking things, hoping to pull off a "hadouken" or "dragon punch." Maybe they did sometimes and felt awfully damn proud of themselves.

Ruby was drunk. She felt like a fallen log, sitting on the forest floor. Sometimes, at certain times of the day, the light shined through the canopy and onto her face. This seemed nice.

Deer and moose walked past often. Once, she saw a porcupine, and once a mother black bear and her two cubs. Ants and termites and other insects made civilizations under her bark, and birds picked at them, happy.

Acknowledgment

The first time I met Lucy, she was living a couple houses down from my wife and me, in the Salt Lake City neighborhood called the Avenues. Being neighborly, she had invited us to a barbeque-style party in her backyard, where she introduced us to her friend Ellen, and we drank gin-and-tonics surrounded by her roommates' mindless friends. At some point in the night I took a bong rip, something that I hadn't done in months and months, and time and light swirled away from me.

It wasn't until a few parties later that we all ended up naked and laughing, taking iPhone photos of each other. Lucy and her new girlfriend, Erin Chuathbaluk, a snowboarder on the U.S. Olympic Team, lost some bet or game and ran across the street butt-ass naked just as a car turned the corner. They darted through the beam of its headlights and hid behind a tree until it passed. Ellen, who had won the game, ran drunk into the street anyway, in a show of solidarity, shrieking shrilly in the warm night, her bare feet slapping the asphalt while my wife and I watched with a group of naked others from the open front door.

Variations on that weekend scene repeated themselves over the months that followed, and we, as a loose group of friends, began to call ourselves "the Avenudes." We found ourselves immersed in a period of easy summertime rowdiness, one in which I could have never predicted my own involvement. I was a few years older than everybody else, and I had begun to think that my days of heavy partying were behind me, so I was surprised that I found myself in situations as seemingly wild as these. However, the contrasting innocence of the gatherings, the earnest disassociation of inebriated nudity from sexuality, as if our group were equal parts frat house and hippie nudist colony, was astonishing. I had never experienced anything like it before.

Maybe that was because nudism, as an idea, had always seemed silly to me, something that I had associated with graying baby boomers who held potluck picnics in the woods, the kinds where you found long pubic hairs in the potato salad. I didn't believe that a man, a man like myself at least, could walk around plain-as-day with naked women, unashamed and unerected, but there I was, doing it.

I had always assumed, that the carefree, peace-and-love attitude was a guise, a way to trick people you didn't know very well into letting you see them naked. In fact, it was a move I had pulled myself. A few years prior, long before the Avenudes, before I was married, back when I had just gotten home from two years as a Mormon missionary and was in a state of confusion so desperate and dark that I would wish it on no other human, I took a late night trip with my friend's ex-girlfriend. I picked her up at her parent's house – she was only 17; I had just turned 22 – and we drove south to the remote, middle part of Utah. There were hot springs there, deep pots of geothermally heated freshwater in the middle of some rancher's field, maybe ten or twelve miles off the freeway, at the end of a dirt road.

It was February, and the night glowed eerily light from the snow that sat thick on the frozen ground. The trip was slow going, even in four-wheel drive, and we reached the springs a little after midnight. No one else was there. I stripped down to my boxers (I had stopped wearing the Mormon garments by then), paused for a moment, and then dropped those too. I snatched a beer from the case and lowered myself into the water. My friend's ex-girlfriend did likewise.

I remember talking as we soaked about how our society's view of sexuality was fucked up, how people couldn't just be naked, couldn't just accept the human body as something simple and innocent, as something other than the object of sexual desire. She agreed, and we admired each other's bodies and our own as the snow began to fall more heavily around us, melting on the surface of the water. We drank more beer, and then I said, "I have a bad idea," and kissed her. She kissed back, and everything crescendoed for fifteen minutes or so.

"I should get out and get dressed," she said with the excruciating timing that I had learned from other girls. "You're

Dane's friend. I feel bad."

"You don't have to get out. It's freezing out there." I splashed my hands on the surface of the water. "It's nice and warm in here." I kissed her neck.

"It really is." She pulled away, reluctantly at first but then determined. "But I should get out." She paddled to the other side of the pool, and lifted herself up into the frigid air. "Where are my clothes? Where's all our stuff?"

"Oh shit," I said. "It's probably covered in snow."

"Where did we put it?" She hugged herself and kicked fresh snow around with her bare feet. Then, "Fuck it. I'm too cold," and she jumped back in.

When she did that, for all my talk of nature and society and nudity not having to be sexual, we fucked.

Believe it or not, that was my first time. 22 years old. The next afternoon, walking around the campus at Brigham Young University, "the Lord's school," and looking at all the other students, I felt awfully proud of myself. I knew something that those virgin dorks didn't. It was if the universe had finally let me in on a secret that everyone I knew had been trying to keep from me my whole life.

But by the first summer of the Avenudes, I no longer harbored such a frantic naïveté. I had travelled a little bit, broken up with more than one girlfriend, and gotten married, settled-the-fuck-down as they say, found a balance. Those were things that I had realized about myself and was okay with. Even so, our parties astonished me. Or rather, my reaction to them did. It wasn't the nudity that amazed me, but the fact that it didn't. Does that make sense? I was overwhelmed by how underwhelmed I was. I felt as though it had been years since the last time I looked in the mirror, and when I finally saw my reflection again I couldn't decide if I recognized myself or not.

But the summer wore down, and Lucy and Erin moved into a house together in another neighborhood. Erin was busy training for competition and Lucy worked a lot, so I saw less of them. I transferred to different university and started classes. I didn't know what Ellen was doing. Even though we had gotten relatively close – we had seen each other naked, after all – I didn't feel like I could hang out with her without everyone else being around too. It just wasn't that kind of arrangement. My wife, Kaia, was the only one with any free time. She was drawing unemployment and spending a lot of time at home or in coffee shops, looking at the internet.

It was December or January when our friends Trout and Lindsey decided they were getting a divorce, and Trout flew from Anne Arbor to Salt Lake in mid-February. He had just finished a two-week stay in the psychiatric ward of some hospital and was visiting for four or five days while Lindsey moved all of her stuff out of their apartment. He slept on our couch those nights. It was Kaia's job to keep an eye on him the whole time because I was at work or class most of those days. Even in the limited time I spent with him, however, Trout did enough damage to twist up my thoughts and keep them misshapen for months afterwards.

For one, he opened himself so completely and honestly to us, and left himself raw and exposed for so long and to such a degree, that my brain was saturated entirely with the terrifying side effects of his brutal, pathetic sincerity. I wouldn't have hosted him if I hadn't loved him, but the hours that we spent together were as long as city blocks and as heavy as mountains. The first thing he did, the very first thing after Kaia and I picked him up from the airport, was to rip off his shirt and show us how he had carved the word "shiteater" in jagged capital letters across his chest with an X-Acto knife. He told stories about the sex that he and Lindsey used to have, about how she would cry and cover her face with a pillow, stories about Craigslist prostitutes he had met in motels, the story of the abortion he had made Lindsey have when they first started dating. He took breaks only to walk up and down the street, pulling his Army surplus jacket tight around him and chain-smoking Marlboro Red 100s, two at a time.

That alone was enough to make my brain feel like a Robt. Williams painting, but the amount of drugs we ingested intensified the effect to the point to where all I could think about was death, sex, marriage, and a lifetime of my own various dishonesties and cruelties.

In opposition to Trout's introspection, which seemed to me to be profoundly lucid, I talked complete nonsense, streams of words that held little meaning and even less importance. My sentences were structured as if to portray everything except what I actually meant, like I expected Trout and Kaia to achieve comprehension from the silhouette of blank space that I left floating before them. I would realize this only after I had finished speaking and, self-conscious, would acknowledge out loud my own clumsy vapidity. This served only to make me even more embarrassed and anxious.

"Christ, Jesus," I said. "I'm an idiot. I'm like a child." Then, with enough foolishness to make the horror of the moment impossible to restore with any accuracy on this printed page, I said, "I should be fucking aborted."

Trout said nothing. I stood from where I was seated on the floor, walked to the bedroom, and laid facedown on the bed. My chest pounded with a tachycardic intensity that frightened me. I tried not to hear Kaia and Trout's voices, but I couldn't block them out. After a few minutes I realized that, because I had shoved my face deep into a pillow and pulled it up around my ears, I wasn't getting any oxygen. I stood again, disrobed, and walked through the kitchen and into the bathroom where I turned on the shower. I stood under the water for a vague amount of time, turning in circles, pacing back and forth for the few steps that the bathtub allowed me, and muttering more nonsense to myself. When the water finally went cold, I sat on the edge of the tub and sobbed until Kaia came to check on me.

"No I'm not okay," I said, something about "having the worst panic attack I ever have." She hugged me, and rubbed my back for another vague amount of time, and then asked if I would be okay if she left for a minute. I said that yes, I would, and I knelt on the tile floor, putting my forehead on the cool porcelain of the tub.

When she came back, Lucy was with her. There wasn't enough room for all three of us in the bathroom, so Kaia left and Lucy knelt down beside me.

"I have something for you," she said, and put a pale blue pill in my hand.

"What is it?"

"It's Klonopin. It will just take that weight off your chest. It takes the edge off."

"Klonopin."

"I think you should take it. It will make you feel better."

"Klonopin."

"You'll be okay, Nate. I get panic attacks all the time, and my doctor gave me this to help."

"You do? Does it?"

"It does."

"Klonopin. Okay."

She left me, and I crawled to the sink and lifted myself up. I put the pill on the back of my tongue and let some water run into my cupped hand. I swallowed it. After a few minutes, my heart and brain slowed down, and I left the bathroom, got dressed, and went into the front room where Kaia and Trout were watching a skate video. Lucy must have just come over to give me the pill and then left immediately.

Neither of them said or did anything, so I said, "we should go in the mountains." They thought this was a good idea, so Kaia drove us to a spot up the hill from our house, where there was a trail that looked over the city, which, despite the afternoon sunlight, was covered by a thick gray-black haze, pollutants trapped in the valley by wintertime inversions. The snow on the trail had been packed down, and we walked along it until we were staring down into the stripped and skeletal groves of scrub oak that lined City Creek Canyon.

I picked up a handful of snow and squeezed it tight like an orange or a grapefruit. The melt-water ran down the sleeve of my coat like fresh juice. Trout asked if I would take a picture of him, and when I agreed he gave me his cell phone and directed me to stand downhill. He took off all of his clothes, right there on city property, in full daylight, and set them in a pile beside him.

"Are you ready?" he asked.

"Yes."

He did a front flip, and landed on his back in the snow.

"I'm going to do it again," and he ran uphill and jumped again. He did this six or seven times, and I took pictures. The best one showed him upside-down, his back and ass-crack and the underside of his ball sac in the air above that ridiculous high-and-tight haircut, a look of total tranquility on his face. He stood and rubbed snow all over his body, on his crotch and across his chest as if he were erasing the letter-shaped scars that were there.

Kaia picked packed a snowball, and mimed biting, like she was pulling the pin from a grenade with her teeth, and she threw it as far as she could, down the southern wall of the canyon.

"I just got baptized, dude," said Trout. "I'm baptized."

My sins weren't washed away so easily. After Trout went home, it took months of therapy to get me right again. Kaia had to do the same thing. I swore off drugs forever, even ganja. I thought I wasn't going to make it out the other side, but the winter finally ended, and the second summer of the Avenudes began.

Lucy and Erin moved back to the avenues, into a 1930s brick house with a big front porch that sat across the street from the Salt Lake City cemetery, the hilly expanse that held the remains of important Mormons who had died since 1848, when Utah was still Deseret, and the West was still wild Mexico. When Pride Weekend came, they threw a celebratory party in which everyone orbited around a few jugs of sweet port wine and a bowl of something called "hunch punch." Along with Brandon McIlvain, the guitarist in Kaia's band

and the brains behind a drone tape label that was too cerebral to be popular, I spent the night playing the role of informal DJ. The songs were mostly rocksteady and dub, songs by Phyllis Dillon, Prince Buster, and the Upsetters that I like to think were the reason that everyone motivated to get naked and climb the elm trees in the front yard, scraping their tender bits on the bark and dropping onto the lawn like fruits of the knowledge of good and evil.

Before the night was over, I had made a proposal to Ellen, who had put her clothes back on and was standing by the sink, drinking water from a ceramic bowl.

"You know, you could come home and party with me and Kaia."

"And what would that entail, exactly?"

"Nah, forget it. I'm drunk."

"No. Say what you were going to say."

"Well, it would entail, you know, a threesome maybe."

"I didn't know that you two would be into something like that. You're a marriage. I love you both. I wouldn't want to mess anything up. Are you sure Kaia's into it?"

"She's as into it as anybody," I said.

"I've never done anything like that before."

"Me neither. Us neither."

"Not tonight. Tell Kaia to text me tomorrow. Not tonight though."

Kaia did, and the event almost worked out a couple of times, but always ended up falling through for one reason or another, and Ellen went to visit her brother in Denver a couple weeks later. We were lying in bed, reading or talking, when we both got the same long text message.

"Hey guys," it said. "Before I left for Denver, Matthew and I talked and we're going to get back together to work things out. Therefore, a threesome is definitely not something I should participate in. Besides that, I am concerned that doing this would put an awkwardness and possible tension on our friendship, which I would hate to have happen. But know that I think you are both beautiful people and I respect and admire you guys. I'll see you both next week... Peace and love til then..."

Sometime in the next couple of weeks, Ellen and I met early in the morning in the park across from all the University of Utah frat houses to play tennis. Neither of us had even touched a racquet since high school, but the basic skills we needed came back quicker than I thought they would. We played two sets. She beat me 6-0 in the first, and 6-4 in the second. Every time the score was Love-15, I would think of John Coltrane's, "A Love Supreme," the mantric album which contained expressions of his devotion to God that had developed after recovering from the famous 1957 heroin overdose. I chanted this line over and over in my head, "A love supreme, a love supreme," and I thought that I could do drugs again if somebody would play tennis with me while I was on them. Except for calling out the score, and declaring whether the ball was in or out, I wouldn't have to talk at all. Instead, I would communicate by focusing all of my mental and physical energy on returning the ball, putting it in the exact right place every time, keeping a simple rally going as long as I could, and knowing that if I made a mistake, if I put the ball wide or into the net, that my opponent would still be happy, because they had won the point.

The Preacher Waylon Jennings

My granddad's dying wish was that I get to hear a sermon given by the famous preacher Waylon Jennings. But then a couple years went by, and still I hadn't gotten around to getting up to Littlefield, Texas, where the preacher was from, and the guilt of it had been starting to get at me. So one groggy morning, after swearing I would never touch another drop of tequila ever again, I started planning the trip. I asked for the time off from my job as a janitor at New Mexico State University, and two weeks later, I left Las Cruces.

I spent the morning driving through Alamogordo and Mescalero and Ruidoso and remembered what my granddad used to say about the preacher. The preacher Waylon Jennings had a powerful voice. He bellowed from the pulpit, pontificating about redemption and the power of love. But he knew how to listen as well. He had avoided death on numerous occasions by being able to hear the still and small promptings of the Lord.

Outside of Roswell, I pulled over to empty my bladder and fill up my truck's tank and look at a map. As I read the names of the towns, I recalled some of the things my granddad had said about Texas, especially West Texas. He had said, "When they named the towns in West Texas, it was almost like they knew that nobody would ever want to visit them anyway." Notrees, Blackwell, Brownwood, Cotton Center, Noodle Dome, Muleshoe, Earth.

I kept driving and eventually crossed the state line. The sun went down behind me so that the western faces of all the monolithic grain silos in Sudan, Texas lit up like their forms had been poured with cement and neon mixed together.

I reached Littlefield around eight. It didn't look like a place that a famous preacher would live, just a dusty, windy pullout off the 84, but it had a McDonald's. I went in and ordered something to eat.

After some time I said in a loud voice, "I think Waylon Jennings would be ashamed by the slow service at his hometown McDonald's.

An employee assured me that my order would be right up, and eventually it came. I carried the tray to a table and sat. I felt like I had a pretty good idea of what Waylon would say about the way the cooks had spit in my Filet-O-Fish, too. I finished my fries and coke and drove down the main drag to the Waylon Jennings RV Park, right next to the ACE Hardware. There were some picnic tables and spots for maybe 15 RVs, but nobody else was camped there.

I got out and walked around. Up toward the front of the park was a plaque with a portrait of the preacher painted on it. He had a short beard and wore a cowboy hat. He looked like a good man. Below the plaque, on the ground, was a concrete slab shaped to look like the state of Texas. The preacher had pressed his boots into the once wet cement, and the prints were there, along with a signature he had drawn with his finger.

At least somebody in this town cared about God's messenger.

I laid out a foam camping pad and my sleeping bag in the bed of my truck. I dreamt that hosts of angels flew around me in big clouds that shifted direction all at once, without any prior indication, like flocks of starlings do.

When I woke, I found that there wasn't a bathroom in the RV park, but I could see one in the run-down city park next to where I was, housed in a little, two-doored cinderblock hut. I hustled over, passing a series of horseshoe pits. Strips of sand with vertical rebar poles stuck into the earth at either end. The sign on the bathroom door said "Restrooms are for Littlefield Horseshoe Club members only," but I tried the handle anyway. Locked. There was a plaque here too, in front of the bathroom. It featured the mounted inaugural first horseshoe thrown out by the preacher Waylon Jennings. I probably would have stopped to gaze upon it longer if I hadn't had to go so badly. I drove back to the McDonald's, my old nemesis, and I shat there.

I didn't think that Waylon Jennings would be happy to know about the vulgar graffiti in the stall.

I said, "Fools' names," shook my head, and spat on the floor, thinking that my granddad would have done the same thing.

Obviously, the Lord had risen up a powerful and holy man in a town that was full of sin, the kind of place that needed it most.

Up the street a way was what looked like the main intersection in town. One corner housed a gas station, but the other three were churches. I parked on the street, and looked at each in turn, not quite sure what denomination the preacher Waylon Jennings subscribed to. I picked the one that looked the fanciest. I thought that the best preacher would probably be in the best church. I approached the front door, where a big good old boy stood in his Sunday best: a white shirt and tie, plus black pants and suspenders, his short hair gelled and parted above a round pink face that looked like a thick and gristly cut of country ham.

I asked if Waylon Jennings would be giving the sermon today.

"No," the man said, slowly, drawn out.

"Do you happen to know where he's preaching today, then?"

The man put his hand on my shoulder and said, "I hate to be the one to tell you this, son, but Waylon Jennings is dead. He died in 2002."

"The preacher is dead?"

"Waylon Jennings wasn't a preacher. He was a country singer. One of the finest country singers America ever knew. Truly one of Texas's native sons."

I said nothing.

He must have seen the distressed look on my face because he said, "If you're looking to hear the Gospel of Jesus Christ, there will be a good meeting today. It won't start for another hour or so, but you're welcome to come inside and wait."

I thanked him, but told him that I thought I'd better be getting back to New Mexico.

I filled my truck with diesel and went back to the RV park. I looked at the portrait of Waylon Jennings again. Sure enough, he looked like a country singer, not a preacher. I put my foot over his boot print in the cement slab shaped like Texas. His feet were much too small for someone chosen by the Lord. Size nine and a half, tops. After checking to make sure that no one was around, I pulled over to the horseshoe club and backed my truck up to the plaque with Waylon Jenning's special horseshoe mounted on it. I left the motor running. In my toolbox, I found a tow chain and hooked it to the tow hitch. The other end I looped around the steel pole that the plaque stood on. I got back in the truck and gunned the engine.

The plaque popped right out of the ground.

I lifted it into the bed of the truck and drove back home.

I didn't call my grandma right when I got back to Las Cruces. I figured I needed a night to sleep on it, but I didn't call her the next day either. When I finally got around to it, I had to have a couple beers and a little nip of tequila before I could work up the courage.

Sitting at her kitchen table, I told her that I had a surprise for her. I went out to my truck and got the plaque.

"What's this?" she asked.

"It's for you," I said.

I told her that the preacher was so moved by Granddad's faith that he sent me back with it. It was to hang on the wall in Granddad's memory.

My grandmother began to weep, and while she did, I got my tools and hung the plaque in the house's entryway.

I stood back to admire my work, and she rose from the table and joined me, taking my rough hand in hers.

She said, "What was the sermon like? What did the preacher look like? Tell me everything."

I told her that the preacher was a good country man. He took off his cowboy hat and set it on the pulpit before he began to speak. He had a long white beard, like God's, and spoke with a voice so beautiful and powerful that you couldn't help but cry when you heard it.

"Your granddad would be proud."

I nodded and gave her a little hug and told her that I had better be off because I had work early in the morning.

Now this was true. I did have work early in the morning, but I didn't go home to bed. Instead, I drove to a little cowboy dive called Rodriguez's Goat, out on the edge of town. I went to the jukebox and found Waylon Jennings there.

The harmonica part of "Lonesome, On'ry, and Mean" played as I took my place at the bar.

I ordered tequila. The first shot I drank was in memory of my granddad, the hard-working man who knew right from wrong. The next was in memory of Waylon Jennings, who the world would never again see face-to-face. All the drinks I had after that weren't in memory of anyone. The rest of that tequila was just for me.

Country Records

Cynthia Godinez drove down to Colorado Springs and showed up at the church where the concert was supposed to be, but when she went inside there was only a bunch of nicely dressed people listening to an old guy give a sermon.

She turned in the pew to the old woman sitting next to her and whispered, "When's Ted Haggard going to play?"

The woman looked at Cynthia's t-shirt and jeans and said, "That IS Ted Haggard."

"Well, is he going to do any country songs?"

The woman pursed her lips.

"Ted Haggard ain't a country singer. He's a preacher. He's up there preachin."

Cynthia thought about this. It didn't make any sense. She had all his records.

The Log Boy Children and the Turtle Dog

I'm in the back making sandwiches when the film crew comes in. Through the window that connects the front and back of house I see the director and some cameramen and the people who wear headphones and hold long poles with microphones at the ends of them. They all follow a dark-haired woman about my age, stylishly dressed with expensive tattoos covering both arms and coming up onto her chest and neck. The woman orders a turkey bacon avocado on focaccia.

Matty, who is at the counter, nervously shifts his gaze from the woman to the cameras. He keeps having to ask her the same questions about her order over and over because he is so anxious.

I make her sandwich, cut it in half, and put a handful of sea salt and vinegar chips in the basket with it. I ring the bell, and Matty takes the sandwich from the window. He calls the woman's name. It is a famous name; one that I recognize. I look at the woman again. The crew films her as she picks up her sandwich from the counter and walks to her table.

Matty looks back at me. I raise my eyebrows. He looks around and then sticks out his tongue and makes a humping motion. But then the door dings, and more customers come in. He stands up straight.

I look at my workstation: my cutting boards, my knives, a refrigerator full of meat.

I look up. This is my chance, I think.

I walk into the employee bathroom and wash my hands. I dry them on my apron, leaving obvious dark streaks on the red cloth. I take it off and hang it on the back of the door.

From the kitchen I can see the woman and her entourage again. They are filming as she eats. Ignoring the tickets that Matty sends back to me, I walk to the dining room.

As I approach her table, the director is saying, "Okay, now shoot from here, with the window in the background, softly, so it's just diffused color in the background."

To the woman I say, "Excuse me."

The cameras turn to me, and the director says, "Jesus fuck."

"I'm sorry," I say. " I just wanted to make sure the sandwich was okay."

"The sandwich?" asks the woman with the famous name.

"I made it."

"It's a wonderful sandwich," says the director, "a real achievement in the field."

The director watches me and looks like he is going to

open his mouth again, but I am quicker.

To the woman with the famous name I say, "I also wanted to tell you that I am a writer. I make sandwiches, but really I am a writer. Short stories, screenplays, that kind of thing. I wanted to offer my services. I mean, not right now. I don't know how much writing you would need for a reality show, but you know. In the future."

"Do you have a card, honey?" asks the woman.

"No. Here. Can I borrow this?" I say, sliding her napkin toward me. I write my name on the napkin, and underneath I write my blog URL and my phone number.

She looks at my name and says, "You wrote 'The Log Boy Children and The Turtle Dog.'"

I nod. It was a story that was published in the *Asscrack Review*, an online journal that doesn't pay its contributors and that no one reads.

"I liked that one," she says.

She picks the napkin off the table and folds it once. She sticks it down her shirt and into her bra for safekeeping, presumably.

I thank her and apologize again to the director and walk back to the kitchen. Matty gives me a look. I start catching up on the sandwich orders. Not remembering that my apron is still hanging in the bathroom, I get mustard all over my pants.

House Party

For years afterward, everybody talked about my big brother like he was some hero, like he was the party king of the universe. I didn't actually see it happen, but I heard them all groan, and when I turned from the kitchen sink, the front of David's Black Sabbath t-shirt was soaked through with blood. They were all gathered, looking at whatever it was he held in his left hand. In his right were Mom's sewing scissors.

"Two snips," said some kid, awed.

I pushed through the crowd.

"What the hell is that thing?"

"It's his nipple."

It sure was, like a spit out bite of someone's country ham.

I looked to David's paled face. He was sweating and

serious, but I could tell from his dark eyes that he was pleased with himself. He punched me on the shoulder and pointed to the thirty rack of Olympia that sat on the kitchen table. I crossed the room and fished one out for him.

This is the part of the story that to this day everybody gets most excited to tell.

He opened the can, popped the severed nipple into his mouth like an aspirin, and threw his head back, downing all twelve ounces of the watery beer.

They cheered, most of them. I stared, and that same kid just kept shaking his head, hypnotized.

"Two snips," he said.

From this, my brother managed to acquire a certain reputation. Everybody knew him as a real tough guy, a crazy-ass son-of-a-bitch, and they loved him for it. He got jobs because of it. In the summer that fell between my freshman and sophomore years of high school, while I was running ladders under Coach Drury's stern eye and the fluorescent lights of Sky View High's basketball gym, preparing for a competitive season still months away, David was framing houses 60 hours a week for 13 dollars an hour. That was big money for a recent high school graduate, especially one who still lived with Mom and Dad and had no rent to pay.

The Camaro came, a 1982, primer gray. It was a machine so fast and so loud that to see a young man like my brother behind the wheel cursed me with a certain discomfort, like watching someone driving an avalanche down the side of a mountain.

Shortly after the car came the girlfriend. Her name was

Allie Sheffield, from Preston, Idaho, just a few miles north of Smithfield, where we lived. She was a year older than I. She wore tight jeans, chopped blue hair, and torn up black t-shirts – Operation Ivy, Anti-Flag, Lars Frederiksen and the Bastards – the uniform of the small town punk rocker. She was the opposite of all the cattlemen and potato farmers and Mormons that filled our neck of the so-called woods. She was the perfect match for my wild brother.

I heard her before I saw her. I was coming down the stairs, in search of my gym bag, stomping and making as much noise as possible as to give fair warning. They answered back with the sounds of frantic shuffling. I heard them scrambling, unlatching from each other to redo the buttons and zippers that they had previously undone. When I found them, they were both sitting upright on the futon, saying nothing, looking mussed and staring casually in different directions.

Every weekend that our parents took their paychecks to the casinos on the Nevada side of Wendover, that same basement became the all-nighter HQ. Though no more body parts were ever cut off, the intensity of these gatherings crescendoed with time. Allie partied almost as hard as my brother did. She was there for every one. So was I.

Accompanying the parties was a seemingly unending supply of alcohol. My brother went to great measures to ensure that everyone knew that he was the supplier. He had paid for it and was sharing it out of the goodness of his heart. They loved him for it, and after a while, there were drugs too: California weed, Adderall, the occasional batch of magic mushrooms. However, these substances were distributed more sparingly and only to a very select after-party crowd. I was almost never invited to these gatherings. Instead I heard about them later from other people. Once, outside the Apollo Burger, James Chase, who was one of the dumbest, meanest, loudest hicks I knew, asked me if I would make an inquiry to David about more bufo.

"What's bufo?"

"Deemster. Dimethyltryptamine, jackass."

Often, when my brother was at work or out driving, I searched for this stash. I fantasized about sharing vodka and pills with my teammates, to pass them out like fun-sized bags of M&Ms, and thus cultivate a more interesting reputation than the one that had stuck to me like a grasshopper to a windshield: B-plus student, decent swingman, David's brother, quiet guy.

It was probably a good thing that I never found that stash, though I often still wonder how our lives would be different if I had.

That was the year that we, the Bobcats, took second in State for our division. David and Allie were both in the stands for the final game. Seeing them stomp and shout like those who find themselves caught up in the rawness of war is one of the few clearly positive memories that I hold of my brother from that period. In fact, that was probably the closest, emotionally speaking, that he and I had been in a year and a half or more. My Bobcats lost the game, obviously, but I can never forget the simple happiness that overcame me as my brother and I briefly occupied the same plane, his face red with adrenaline and fury, cheering for me, saying my name even.

Toward the middle of my junior year, when David finally ended what had been a slow but steady decline, he hit the rockiest of bottoms.

After a Saturday night of partying somewhere, he was rushing to get Allie home before the twelve o'clock curfew her father had set.

There was an accident.

In the intersection by the Maverik gas station, David and Allie and that primer-gray Camaro blasted through a red light, the only stop light in Richmond, Utah, like it wasn't even there, smashing up a Honda Civic on the way and killing the driver, a 20-year old college student named Elaine Crandall. The reports would later state that Allie had screamed, pleading with David to stop the car. Instead, he kept right on driving to her house. He had been high on a mix of Xanax and one-third of a bum jug of Carlo Rossi sangria.

My brother was still in bed, yet to confront the imminent hangover, when the police came to the house the next morning. I pushed the lawn mower into the front yard and found the cops there, staring at the mangled front bumper and crumpled hood. They seemed less perplexed that I was about the damage, which I was just now seeing for the first time.

"Is this your car, son?" one of them asked.

"It's my brother's," I said, immediately wishing that I hadn't.

The legal costs and the settlement were high, higher than I could comprehend at the time. Even my parents realized that the amount of money David owed was more than any Nevada slot machine or one-dollar Idaho scratch card would ever pay out. The house had to be sold, and we had to move to an apartment complex in Logan, seven miles south.

The judge sentenced David to five years at the Utah State Prison at Point of the Mountain. I cried. My mom and dad cried. David, the person I had once seen cut off his own nipple without flinching, cried.

"Can you imagine," he said as I hugged him goodbye, "knowing you will be punished for something you can't even remember?"

Allie did not attend the hearing.

I didn't see her again for almost a month. It was the day we were supposed to have finished moving out and cleaning up, but we weren't even close. I was standing in the garage with my ear buds in, moving boxes around and applying long strips of packing tape. The sun silhouetted her in the garage door where she stood watching me, apparently hesitant to cross the threshold. I stopped my music.

"Hey, Allie," I said. "How are you?"

"Oh you know. What about you?"

I nodded to the boxes around me.

"Weird."

She nodded.

"I'm not interrupting you, am I?"

"Not at all."

"Are you sure? Because I can come back later or whatever."

"It's really no problem. This is hopeless anyway. I need a break."

"Well, okay." She hesitated, pulling at her torn up t-shirt that gave glimpses of her stomach. "I have a favor to ask."

"What is it?"

"I'm not sure how to get a hold of David yet, so I thought I'd better come talk to you before you moved down to Logan.

I wonder if you would pass along a message for me."

"I could give you the address you can write him at, if you want."

She frowned and said, "No. I think it would be better if someone told him in person, and I'm not ready to go do it myself."

"What's the message?"

The message was that Allie was pregnant.

I visited David once every one or two months. It was a three-hour drive, but I didn't mind. I wanted to visit more often, and I felt guilty about not doing so, but when I finally got there we never had had much to say to each other. The scratched up, bulletproof glass between us didn't exactly enhance the brotherly experience. I didn't know how to bring up the things that I needed to say. I figured there were a few years to go before I would have to. I hoped that as time passed something would occur to me, but nothing ever did. Allie never said anything either, although she visited him far less than I did.

She and I had started spending time together about a week after the day that she came by the house. We vented to each other, helped each other through some things, became vulnerable, became close. After baby Reggie was born, we started dating. Eventually, we moved in together. We had an apartment just south from the Utah State University campus. I was two years into a bachelor's of science in geology, worked 25 hours a weeks washing dishes, and was looking forward, always forward, to the moment that things would suddenly become easier. We had big plans. We were going to get married, Allie and I. I was going to adopt my brother's kid as my own. I never said it out loud, but I had it in my mind that I would do all the things David should have done if he hadn't gone to prison.

Then, after three years and two months, a surprise to us all, David got out on good behavior. He spent the six months after his release in a halfway house. I didn't visit him while he was there. Mom and Dad did a couple of times, and when he called them to let them know that he was done, they drove to Salt Lake to pick him up. Meanwhile, Allie and I waited at my parent's apartment. Our task was to get a bedroom ready for him, cook dinner, tie 'round the proverbial yellow ribbon.

I can't speak for Allie, but I was scared, anxious, and, for some selfish reason or another, a little pissed off. We would have no choice now but to do what had to be done, to say the words that should never fall between brothers no matter how distant the making of their lives.

I took the chicken casserole from the oven, and we sat at the table in silence. Reggie was in my parents' bedroom, asleep.

It was 34 minutes later – I know because I couldn't manage to draw my eyes from the clock for more than a minute or two at a time – that David came grinning through the front door. He looked good, better than I had imagined he would, though he had lost 20 or 30 pounds and was missing his two front teeth. At first glance, he looked hard, like an actual ex con. New tattoos peaked out from beneath his shirtsleeves, but his eyes shined with life.

Allie and I stood to greet him, and he pulled us both in for a tight hug.

"Congratulations, you two."

"For what?" Allie asked, glancing sideways at me.

"For the life that you have made together. Mom and Dad told me in the car on the way here. I can't think of anything better than for two of the people I love most to be together and happy."

"We thought that you might be upset," I said.

"No, man. I wouldn't get upset over a thing like that. How could I?"

Images flashed through my head of a past incarnation of my brother, one who always found a reason to crack someone in the jaw or kick them in the ribs.

As if reading my mind, he said, "Things are different now. I'm different now. I really think that I've figured some things out. Being in prison sucked. Prison is horrible. But I think that I can take enough good from it to be able to regard it as a positive experience over all. You can make any experience a positive experience."

"Oh man, you got right with Jesus didn't you? You found religion."

He laughed.

"Not exactly. I have found my path though, so to speak."

"And what's that?"

Allie interrupted us.

"Why don't you tell us about it over dinner, David? The casserole's almost cold."

He looked at the food on the table, and shook his head.

"I should have told you. There's no way you could have known."

"What's that?" she asked, gritting her teeth, knowing that he might say any number of things.

"I'm vegan now."

"Vegan?"

"Right. You all go ahead and eat. I'll go out and get something a little later."

Not knowing whether to feel guilty or offended, the rest of us ate. David talked and talked. The last cellmate he had had, a guy named Bill Porter, had been sentenced to 11 years. Porter was a known supporter of the Animal Liberation Front, those black-clad zealots who are famous for raiding mink farms and had recently found themselves on the FBI's domestic terrorist watch list. Bill had never raided anything, according to David. He had just been pulled over for speeding. The police had searched his truck and found bolt cutters and a crowbar. Burglary tools. This was enough, along with the right words from the right lawyer to the right judge, to get him put away for a long time. Instead of reforming him, prison only radicalized him further. With nothing else to think or talk about, he had turned David into an anarchist.

David spoke without seeming to ever stop for a breath, as if he were to lose momentum, other, less pleasant memories of prison would surface. He told us all about his new beliefs: libertarian socialism, labor rights, direct action, Earth First, the Paris Commune, the Zapatistas, and on and on.

"Americans are tricked into living shitty lives, working, going to school, going to church, taking prescribed Adderall and Xanax," – we all winced – "forced to into an unnatural productivity that exists so they will desire to buy stupid shit and feed more money into the beast that enslaves them. Satan laughing spreads his wings, man. We have to tear it down. Anarchism, a complete new start, is the only way to achieve freedom and peace."

Finally, he paused.

Allie said, "You think lawlessness will create a utopia?"

"There is no such thing as a utopia. There is only the planet. And I need to fight for the planet."

That was the second to last time that I saw my brother, and the last time that anybody else did. He disappeared for the next few years into what he would have referred to as "the underground." This meant that I spoke with him less than I had when he was in prison: I didn't speak to him at all.

Life marched on without him. I finished school but didn't get the oil company job I had been dreaming of. We moved to Santa Barbara where I started the job that I still have today, leading environmental remediation projects under the direction of the US Navy. Reggie's younger half-brother, Matthias, was born.

We had little occasion to speak of David. I almost never even thought of him. I had trained myself not to see him when I looked at my boys. David's character had become that of a specter, a misremembered dream. His prison-born philosophies had faded from my mind even faster than he had. The what and how of my life where such that there was no room for them. I raised my kids, loved my wife, played a game of basketball with a small group of my colleagues every now and then. I took up golf. I took up cycling.

Then, last fall, The FBI contacted me. Two agents, looking comically like they do in the movies, waited for me in the parking of my work, wearing not only their dark suits, but the somber look of interrogation on their faces.

"Arturo Castro?" one of them asked.

"Yes."

They showed their badges.

"Why don't we have a chat?"

Standing there in the parking lot, leaning against the driver's door of my Dodge truck, I answered their questions. No, I hadn't seen my brother. I didn't know of his whereabouts. I had no way of contacting him. I would let them know the second that he contacted me. They seemed to believe me.

The weeks passed, during which I attempted to live as normally as possible, though I had never been the type remotely likely to arouse the suspicions of the bureaus or agencies. It occurred to me that the paranoia I felt was the same sensation that David had years ago tried to express with his stories and seemingly extremist hypotheses.

The night I woke up to the noise coming from the garage, I was sure they were raiding me. I walked downstairs in my bare feet, my hands clearly visible so that no mistakes could be made, so that no shots would be fired. It did not occur to me until I was swinging open the door and stepping down into the garage that my intruder might not be linked to the FBI at all, that it might actual be a real-life burglar. I balled my fists.

The figure, hunched over the tool bench, whipped around to face me. He'd let his beard grow long over his gaunt face, and his long hair was dreadlocked, but it was unmistakably David.

"Hey Arturo," he said.

"Shit. I almost fucking killed you."

"Don't call the cops, okay? Let's just talk for a minute."

"Did you come to see Reggie?"

"What? No. Sorry. I didn't mean to make so much noise. I

thought I'd just hang out until you woke up."

"You can't be here, man. They'll fuck me too."

"I know, bro. I know. The last thing I want is for you to get in trouble. My plan is to leave first thing in the morning. But I need your help with something first. Will you help me, man?"

"What did you do? Why is the FBI looking for you?"

"You're not going to call them right? If you're going to call them, that would be bad."

I sighed and said, "No I'm not going to call them, David."

"Okay." He seemed to relax, if only slightly. "I'll tell you. I'm a suspect in a terrorist case, of course, a crime that shouldn't be terrorism at all. It was only arson, really."

"Jesus."

"Well, there are these police officers in Santa Fe who a month or so ago choked a homeless woman to death in an alley. They claimed that she was resisting arrest and that she was violent, but she committed no crime other than being homeless and mentally ill. She wasn't dangerous. Not nearly as dangerous as those two bastard-ass cops. The two of them have a history of brutality and abuse, but they have never once been held accountable for their actions. They got put on paid administrative leave. One of them, Officer Francisco Pereira, took the opportunity to go on a vacation to Maine with his family. He killed an innocent person and got to go on a fucking vacation as a result. It's fucked."

"This speech sounds like you practiced it in front of a mirror, David."

"Do you want to know, or not?"

"Yeah, yeah. Okay."

"Anyway, somebody found out where this cop lived, and while he was out of town they set fire to his house. Pretty fucking radical move. Pretty fucking heroic, depending on who you ask. The authorities are calling it domestic terrorism."

"So how are you tied to this?"

"Yeah. As the arsonist was fleeing the scene, a bystander who happened to be walking his dog at three AM or whatever saw the glow of the flames and grabbed the dude. There was a scuffle, and his ski mask got pulled off and his shirt got torn. He had dreadlocks."

"So what? A lot of people have dreadlocks."

"He also only had one nipple."

"Jesus Christ."

"I'm in the system, man. I'm known to those fuckers for being politically active. They want to take me down. This is their perfect opportunity."

"You're not going to like what I'm going to ask."

"What?"

"Where have you been this whole time?"

He looked startled. "That wasn't the question I was expecting."

"Because I've been here, David. With the family."

He returned my stare for a moment, then said, "Aren't you going to ask me if I did it?"

The favor that he wanted me to do for him was a significant one. He was going to make a run for Mexico, to Chiapas, he said, to unyoke himself from the heartache of life. To do so, he needed some money. But he didn't want any of mine. He had some of his own, plenty in fact; he just had to get his hands on it.

After the sun rose and I told Allie that I had been called away on a last minute business trip, I drove a few blocks to the 7-Eleven where I had told him to meet me. We pointed ourselves in the direction of Richmond, Utah.

It was night by the time we got close, the headlights of trucks in Sardine Canyon blinding me. It wasn't late enough, he said, so we ate at Angie's Diner in Logan. I relished the nostalgia that accompanied the meal. He ate the few vegan menu items that there were- salad, French fries, water – quickly, his Utah Jazz ball cap pulled low over his eyes. When I had finished my pie, I looked up at him, and he nodded.

We parked down the block from our old house and walked. All the lights were off. We hopped the side fence and snuck through the backyard, only illuminated by an ugly sliver of moon. I almost stepped into a swimming pool that I hadn't been expecting to find. Whoever lived there was doing far better than our family ever had in those days of yore when the backyard was all dry weeds filled with grasshoppers and rattlesnakes.

When I turned around, David had jimmied the back door open. He stood by it, waiting.

"How the fuck did you do that so quickly?" I whispered.

He put his finger to his mouth and looked stern.

David moved silently, and I took care to attempt the same. And though I felt clumsy and self-conscious, I was able to move easily through the nighttime hallways. The layout of the house had not changed. It was a game. I was a teenager again, sneaking back upstairs after getting on the internet late at night on the family computer. Despite the tachychardic frenzy of my heart and the greasy sweat shining on my palms,

I was enjoying myself, grinning even. So much so in fact, that I didn't even register that David was leading us right to my childhood bedroom.

The door was shut.

He eased it open.

I have since dreamt about that moment many times. In these dreams, he opens the door and a teenage girl in cotton panties and a too-big t-shirt sits up in bed, wide-eyed, hair wild. He jerks his head in her direction, and I clamp my hand over he mouth before she can scream.

The scene plays over and over like that.

Of all the dreams, this is the least terrifying.

Thank God that my adventure with David that night didn't turn out like the nightmares that have stuck with me. Instead, we found that my old bedroom had been turned into a craft room. David clicked on his headlamp, skirted a folding table topped with scrapbook supplies, and went to the far corner where my dresser used to be. He cocked back and punched his gloved fist straight through the drywall. Shoulder deep, he fished around for a moment before coming up with a manila envelope. He checked it. Enough money to get him to Mexico, even after he paid me for the gas from the trip.

I left David in Salt Lake City, just across from the Mormon Temple, which looked like a haunted castle in the middle of the night. That was the last time I expected to ever see him.

We embraced.

He said, "Now you know where I hid the drugs all those years. I redid the wall every time. Painted over it and everything. I was a pro at that construction work, man. I should have stuck with it, I guess. Blue collar shit."

"Mexico," I said.

He's gone, but the dreams go on. In the worst ones, there are two children asleep in the room. A breeze blows over them from an open window. They look peaceful, very much like my own boys, and David and I move quietly as to not wake them, the sounds of their breathing rising over the pitter-patter of our felony in progress.

I wake in a panic each time. I stand from my bed and go down the hall to make sure that two strange men, brothers long separated by space and time but connected eternally by a few liters of blood and less than half a lifetime of shared memories, aren't tiptoeing past my unconscious sons.

What Fucking Up Feels Like

I feel like I fucked up, maybe. Like I shouldn't have made such a big deal about my girlfriend cheating on me. Because I actually don't care if my sexual partners have sex with other people.

She looks hot as fuck in this park. This park was supposed to be a safe, neutral place. Her new haircut; no bra under her tank top.

She's yelling, "YOU GET OFF ON THIS SHIT, DON'T YOU?"

She's yelling, "YOU LOVE GIRLS THROWING THEMSELVES AT YOU, BEGGING YOU!"

It's the dishonesty I care about. The double standard. I can't explain that nothing about this situation gets me off, so I stand up and try to walk away. She tries to kiss me.

It felt like fucking up last spring when I got her pregnant.

One night right before her abortion we were out drinking with friends and I thought, she looks so hot I want to get her pregnant again.

In the park, she says, "Why can't you just SEE me? Why don't you understand that in adult relationships you have to work through shit to become closer?"

And like an asshole I say—though I'm immediately proud of myself for not visibly losing my cool—"You don't get to talk to me about 'adult relationships.'"

And in the park she screams, "FUCK YOU! I AM an adult!"

And even though her face is all scrunched up and she's crying, I think, goddamn she's so beautiful. Goddamn, I fucked up.

But I also think, talk to me once you've been married. Talk to me once you've gotten divorced.

I'd spent the previous night with Sienna, Sienna with the buzzed head and a cute-as-fuck crooked front tooth. Everything stayed PG-13, but we snored at each other, and it felt nice to wake up next to her.

It didn't exactly feel like fucking up.

Here's what did feel like fucking up though:

A few hours before going to the park I was hanging out with my mom. As a 30-year old man, I had to admit to my mom that I had started smoking again because I was a sad piece of shit. She was in town, and we stopped for gas on the way to the movies. I went inside the gas station and came out with a pack of yellows.

We were driving, and my mom said, "Here, let me see

that pack real quick." Then she handed it out the window to a homeless person.

It all fucking feels like fucking up. Every bit of it. The way I had stupidly brushed aside the absolute, indisputable fact that my girlfriend had been texting nudes to this stupid nightclub DJ in Denver. Just like it had felt like fucking up when I had looked at her phone while she was in the shower. I thought maybe the two fuckups would cancel each other out or something. It feels like fucking up to have thought that.

It had felt like fucking up every time she'd gotten drunk and emotional and had run away, and I had chased down the street after her, leaving my friends sitting bewildered there at the bar.

It had really, really felt like fucking up when I had kissed my housemate a little. This was before I'd found out that I'd been cheated on. It feels like fucking up not to mention this in the park, with all my talk of honesty, but this is my time to be self-righteous. Feeling self-righteous feels like fucking up, too.

It feels like fucking up every time I smell the dirty mop-water and bathroom cleaner smell of the stupid bar that I go to all the fucking time.

It feels like fucking up every time I get so trashed on Rainier and well whiskey that I scratch on the 8-ball over and over.

Every time I buy coke as the bars are closing.

Every time I go after hours to unlock the bookstore where I work and hang out there.

Every time I blow lines off the display tables.

Every time I can't express my stupid feelings and my stupid intentions.

Every time I can't keep my goddamn idiot mouth shut.
It feels like fucking up to write this.
And I hope it feels like fucking up to read it, too.

The Way Cities Feel to Us Now

Bad luck clung to you like a tick to the belly of a dog.

This started, as best you can remember, the moment that the road beneath your boots turned from dust to asphalt. The song you made up marks this moment in your memory.

You repeated the lines to yourself over and over so that you would not forget them. Later, when the sun was down and you were sitting along by your campfire in the mud on the chigger-infested bank of the Apalachicola River you started pick it out on your guitar, still feeling hopeful and romantic about the travels ahead. You sang, "where the dirt road ends/ where the pavement begins/that's where you'll find me with a broken heart." Then your low E string snapped and you swore.

From then on, from Chattahoochee to Albuquerque, it was one thing after another: wasp stings, dirty campsites, poison oak, blisters, cops, cops, cops. You took bad acid in Lincoln. Homebums stole your guitar outside of Oklahoma City. The only reason certain bad things didn't happen to you is because worse ones did. This was the rule, and there was only one exception. Only once did it happen the other way around.

You had eater nearly half of a Domino's pizza and maybe four plates of salad from Food Not Bombs in Denver. Of course, it had all come out of a dumpster somewhere, but you didn't mind. You were used to it. You ate out of dumpsters almost every day, and you had never gotten sick. Except for this time.

You were standing on a southbound I-25 onramp when your stomach told you that something was very wrong. The pain doubled you over, but you fought through it, and soon enough a white Chevy pickup truck pulled over. Amazed that you were actually getting a ride for once in your miserable life, you hopped in.

The driver was an ugly cowboy, three quarters drunk, his thin hair plastered to his pockmarked brow with seat. A gray Stetson hat sat on the dash, facing forward so that you had to look out over it to see where the truck was headed, like it, this gross and archaic symbol of the old west's backwardness, was now in charge of the journey and you were only following along wherever it led.

The stomach pains came back strong, but you gritted your teeth and they subsided as quickly as they had come on. You didn't ask to be let out of the truck. The ugly cowboy was going all the way to Fort Garland, and you didn't want to miss the opportunity. Lord knows chances like this had been too few and much too fucking far between.

You held it, and you felt proud of yourself.

Everything was going better than expected until about Castle Rock, when the ugly cowboy reached across and started caressing your thigh, and you could see his Wranglers pitching themselves into a horrible tent.

"Oh shit," you said.

And suddenly, you did.

The stink rose like a cloud of mustard gas. The ugly cowboy gagged audibly and withdrew his claw.

The Chevy's tires kicked up gravel and dust.

He left you standing on the shoulder, and you left him with upholstery so soiled that the windows steamed up.

But that was a far, far, away then, and this is right fucking now. And right fucking now you know your luck has shifted. You're in Tucson, where you've spent the evening wandering up and down Fourth Street until stopping to listen to a busker: this beautiful rainbow oogle on a beat up mandolin.

And after a couple songs he takes your hand in his and leads you to a place he knows, an ink-dark corner of the parking lot behind the Green and Black Café.

That's where you are now. You are getting the best blowjob of your life. You know that this means things are changing.

That bad luck built up in you until there was no more room to hold it.

You are about to cast it from you like a broken curse.

You are going to purge.

You are going to shoot the bad luck out and into a pal puddle on the cracked and broken asphalt.

END

Acknowledgments

Special Thanks to Mallory Smart, Bulent Mourad, Rachel Pfeffer, Liz Whitman, Bart Schaneman, Adam Gnade, Noah Cicero, Brendan Wells, Tanner Ballengee, Maxim Popoff, Simon Kugel, Dillon Cramer, Zeke Foerster, Hopyard Mathieson, Jacob Spetzler, Sienna Zorigian, Peter Jones, Collin Tracy, Emily Centipede, Ethan Cohen, Leah White, Nick Gregorio, Rane Miranda, Jason Bahr, Caitlin Bahr, Felix Bahr, Donnette Perkins, and everyone who's come to the readings and shows. Thanks to the editors of the journals and magazines in which many of these stories originally appeared.

Nathaniel Kennon Perkins lives in Boulder, CO, where he works as a bookseller. He is the author of the short novel, Cactus, and the ongoing literary zine series, Ultimate Gospel. His creative work has appeared in Triquarterly, High Country News, the Philadelphia Secret Admirer, decomP magazinE, Pithead Chapel, Timber Journal, and others. He runs Trident Press.

www.ingramcontent.com/pod-product-compliance
Lightning Source LLC
Chambersburg PA
CBHW021702110726

47902CB00007B/2032